# NEIGHBORS *of*
# *Nothing*

T0160489

# NEIGHBORS *of* *Nothing*

**JASON OCKERT**

DZANC
BOOKS

**DZANC BOOKS**

1334 Woodbourne Street
Westland, MI 48186
www.dzancbooks.org

*The characters and events in this book are fictitious. Any similarity to real persons, living or dead, is coincidental and not intended by the author.*

NEIGHBORS OF NOTHING

Copyright © 2013, text by Jason Ockert.

All rights reserved, except for brief quotations in critical articles or reviews. No part of this book may be reproduced in any manner without prior written permission from the publisher: Dzanc Books, 1334 Woodbourne Street, Westland, MI 48186.

The following stories have been previously published, some in slightly different form: "Into the Dead" as "Calicoed" in *H_NGM_N*; "Jakob Loomis" in *Oxford American* and *New Stories from the South*, edited by Kathy Poires (Algonquin Books, Chapel Hill, 2007) and *The Best American Mystery Stories*, edited by Otto Penzler (Houghton Mifflin, New York, 2007); "Still Life" in *One Story*; "Everyday Murders" in *storySouth*; "Insectuality" in *Ecotone*; "Max" in *The Iowa Review*; "Minute Minute" in *Indiana Review*; "Piebald" in *Mid-American Review*; "Sailor Man" in *Post Road*; and "Echo" in *Witness*.

Book design by Steven Seighman.

Published 2013 by Dzanc Books

ISBN: 978-1938604478
First edition: November 2013

This project is supported in part by awards from the National Endowment for the Arts and Michigan Council for Arts and Cultural Affairs.

Printed in the United States of America

10   9   8   7   6   5   4   3   2   1

*For D, G, and J*

# CONTENTS

Into the Dead                1

Jakob Loomis                 4

Still Life                  25

Everyday Murders            44

Insectuality                66

Max                         79

Minute Minute              102

Piebald                    128

Sailor Man                 152

Echo                       181

It is winter and the new year.
Nobody knows you.
Away from the stars, from the rain of light,
You lie under the weather of stones.
There is no thread to lead you back.
Your friends doze in the dark
Of pleasure and cannot remember.
Nobody knows you. You are the neighbor of nothing.

—from "Elegy for My Father," by Mark Strand

# NEIGHBORS *of*
## *Nothing*

# INTO THE DEAD

My old man and a group of his codger friends are biking the Appalachian Trail. This, apparently, is Guinness-worthy. The average age of the bastards is something really old I can't recall. If he makes it to the other side his name will be noted in the book.

I'm here in his house next to the phone. The old coot has been riding incommunicado—no technological doohickeys—and he's due into Hellfire, West Virginia any time now. He's going to use a payphone and call his wife to check in, let her know everything is fine. His wife's the one with everything planned out. My father and I being estranged doesn't sit well with her. She tells me, "If only you could know the kind of person I have come to know and love." She's talking about a Renaissance-type Recovered-man capable of leading a platoon of brittle-legged yahoos on mountain bikes through rocky terrain and into record breaking immortality. And she asks, "Do you know why he's doing this? Do you?"

Earlier this evening his wife called my house where I'd been ironing creases out of a pair of cotton pants. She pretended to be all hopped-up and bewildered. Apparently, her cat had run away and she was afraid of a Doberman a few doors down. She couldn't leave, though, and miss my father's call. By the time I arrived she was standing in warmer clothes than the late spring weather required, half in porch light, half in darkness, clutching the cordless phone and some loose-leaf paper. I was to make *Missing Cat* signs, she explained, and then said a few complimentary things about her calico-colored cat named Moonshine. She was going to have a look around the neighborhood. "If the phone rings," she said, shoving the gray phone into my unwilling arms, "for Heaven's sake, answer it." I'd started in with protests until she got all adder-eyed and grumpy and scurried away, saying, "Don't break my heart."

So, I'm settled in the kitchen where a glass of iced tea is waiting next to a newspaper clipping—poorly clipped—from the local rag. The article I'll not read is accompanied by a picture of my father who is leaning against his mountain bike with a triumphant grin crawling out of his muffled beard. He is wearing some cofangled helmet and biker shorts sizes too small and this image sends me to the sunflower-festooned papered wall to unplug the phone line from the cordless adapter cradle. Let him wonder why it's busy.

Cowering behind the phonebooks on the high shelf I root out some bourbon I figured I'd find. He stashes it just where he used to stash it. The stuff melts the ice in the tea. Then I set to work on those *Missing Cat* flyers trying to describe what calico looks like.

There are kinds of kindness better suited for people different than my father and me. My father's wife should squeegee the bigness of her swollen heart into the mouths of the needy, neglected children, maybe veterans of foreign wars. Instead, she's fanning his charade, churning away like a lunatic on a stationary bike.

I suspect that my father already called his wife earlier tonight. He drummed up some customary pleasantries while she worked out the details of her reunion plan. Told him to call back in an hour; Moonshine had slipped out the back door. Then she called me. Those pants were bad. Even the wrinkles had wrinkles. She thinks my father and I can be cajoled into reconciliation. She thinks he's capable of articulating the significance of this gesture. He is biking the Appalachian Trail in order to showcase the possibility of cycling out the bad blood that previously existed between us and transfuse some good now, starting this coincidental instant on the phone.

Of course, I'll let his call catch the dial tone.

From the kitchen window I see Moonshine wending through the petunia. My best guess is that my father's wife is crouching behind the hedge, eavesdropping, too curious to miss the moment. Sheer yellow-flowered curtains billow in the light breeze. I drink my tea slowly, appreciating it, letting my father's wife really feel the burn in her legs, writing, *He looks like swirled butterscotch and fudge.*

When I'm good and done I pretend I hear a quick ring, pick up the phone, and speak proudly into the dead to my old man.

# JAKOB LOOMIS

Therm is in the woodshed rubbing gasoline on his bloodstained sneakers when he sees a handcuffed man break from the woods and amble toward the house. Hefting an axe, Therm calls out, and the man, surprised, arms defeated behind his back, freezes.

The men consider each other over the short distance of semi-mowed backyard lawn in the cool pre-rain breeze. The mower hunkers to the bloodied ground between the woodshed and the house. For a moment the men feel the weight of their guilt, and then the moment breaks.

"What the hell are you doing?" Therm asks, stepping forward with the axe.

"Hoping I could get a little water," the handcuffed man says, nodding to a green hose heaped next to the house.

Therm is a big man with broad shoulders and a measurable gut. He isn't a fighter, but he can defend himself if he has to. Especially with an axe. And if his potential opponent is handcuffed. There is nothing threatening about the restrained man; he is a foot shorter than Therm and has wiry hair, sun-browned skin, and a long chin. What makes Therm uncomfortable are the man's eyes. There is something off about them—not crossed exactly, just crooked.

"Looks like you've gotten yourself into some trouble," Therm says, squaring himself against the other man.

The man raises his eyebrows, cocks his head back, and gazes down his chin at the bloodied patch of lawn. "You too," he responds.

"What, that? That was an accident. I hit a snake," Therm says.

"A lot of blood for a snake."

"A nest of them, I guess."

Therm was new to his house, just out of a wasted marriage to a woman who cheated on him with several of the felines in a low-budget theater troupe who performed an interpretation of *Cats* in town for a season. Therm discovered a long whisker on the stairs and thought nothing of it because of Molly and Digger, both big, nervous cats. Then whiskers started turning up everywhere. Whiskers on the love seat, in the hamper, next to the lava lamp, in the trunk of their Suburban: brown, blond, green. Green, of course, made Therm suspicious. Then, because his wife considered herself an amateur actress, and because he wanted to make an effort to understand her passions more, Therm bought two tickets to the show. He was shocked by the performance; the unitard-clad men with unrealistic bulges in their crotches meowing and fawning across the stage didn't impress him. When the green cat came out, Therm's wife had emitted a low purr of sorts, and that was that. Therm didn't make a fuss. She kept the property, he was rewarded a significant check her family could afford if the reason for the divorce stayed discreet. Molly and Digger remained with the wife.

Therm moved south and into the country where he wouldn't be bothered. He was a contract cartographer and worked at the drafting table he erected in the family room. The missing boy, though he wasn't missing yet, let his pet parrot free. The bird flew to Therm's property, landed in a tree infested with gnats, and started squawking. Therm went outside to look at the pretty bird thinking that maybe parrots were native to this neck of the woods. He tried talking to it. He said, "Hi birdie, birdie, hi, birdie, birdie," and so on. The parrot squawked and sometimes bobbed its head. Therm retired back inside for work on the rivers of the Middle East. The parrot kept at its racket. Therm tried to ignore the bird. He put cotton in his ears. Music didn't help. Outside, he talked reason; "Okay, bird, enough. Shoo or shut-up, birdie, birdie." The parrot preened its feathers and continued screeching. Gnats were abundant. Therm tossed rocks. When he called Animal Control they said that a noisy bird wasn't an animal they considered a threat. He was put on hold for a minute. When the operator came back, he said to Therm, "We'll send a rescue squad over immediately. You're in grave danger. Whatever you do, don't let it hit you on the head with its lethal crap. You wouldn't believe how many people die from parrot dookie every year." There was laughter in the background. Therm hung up.

All that night the parrot made its noise. The next day, more of the same. Therm couldn't concentrate on the complicated tributaries of the Euphrates River. He took a long hike and disrupted a fox chasing a rabbit. The fox hid behind a slash pine and angrily glared at Therm as the rabbit dashed away. A half-mile from home, Therm heard the parrot. When he listened hard, Therm detected a squawking pattern that he imitated for a while for fun. Then the pattern broke.

In bed that night, trying to ignore the bird, Therm thought of Madeline, his ex-wife. They had been an attractive couple in college, lost their virginity together, wrote their own marriage vows, and enjoyed the mall on late afternoons. *Damn her for throwing that all away*, he thought.

In the morning, Therm started drawing irrational parallels between the parrot and Madeline and frequently yelled for Maddy to *pipe down* or *put a sock in it*. This made him feel a little better.

The bird kept calling and eating gnats and staring at Therm with sidelong eyes as Therm stood below it with the old rifle his grandfather had left him in the will. Therm figured he'd scare the damned thing by firing near its head. But the parrot didn't budge, just twittered uncomfortably and changed to a higher pitch. A couple shots later, Therm knew he wasn't trying to warn the bird anymore. Still, he couldn't get a bead on the multicolored beast as it hopped from branch to branch.

At Food 4 U, Therm bought fruit he knew his ex-wife enjoyed; grapes, strawberries, and bananas. On the front door of the store was a black-and-white picture of the missing boy, smiling, that the clerk had just posted. Therm paid for his food. At home, he diced the fruit and laced it with rat poison from a bottle he kept under the sink. He placed the concoction on a paper plate and set it on a stump beneath the trees. He hid himself in the shed with the door cracked and waited all afternoon for something to happen. The bird squawked. A squirrel nosed the fruit but left it alone. Just before the sun set, the parrot glided down to the fruit and investigated. It ate a grape and spit it out. It overturned the paper plate and shat. Therm rushed out of the shed with the axe, but the parrot was too quick and settled itself back in the tree.

Therm couldn't get Madeline out of his head as he smudged the Tigris River. She had really whipped him good. She never let him eat spicy foods and complained when he walked around the living room naked. She wore wool socks to bed and rubbed her feet over his legs at night. Some mornings, he'd wake up with a rash. *Then she sleeps with a clowder of cat-men? She didn't even like sex*, he thought. She had a bevy of excuses when he was in the mood; *I'm tired, I've got cramps, Molly's in heat, I just washed these sheets*, and so on. Supposedly, one of the actors had a SAG connection and Madeline was going to be an extra in some romantic comedy coming out next fall. *She screws me*, Therm thought, *finds success doing something she loves, and I'm here with the loudest parrot in the world.*

Therm decided to call Madeline's house and let the parrot bark its brains out over the answering machine.

In the morning, Therm went to Widgit's Hardware and asked a Widgit employee for the most powerful nozzle they had. Next to the register was the black-and-white picture of the missing boy, smiling.

"Are we talking fifty feet?" the Widgit employee asked.

"A hundred and fifty," Therm replied.

"That's a specialty item, it'll cost you."

"Charge it."

Therm attached the high-powered nozzle to the hose and tested it against the side of the house. It chipped the paint. Satisfied, Therm unwound the hose and stalked up next to the parrot-tree. The parrot quieted and watched suspiciously. Therm let it rip. The parrot was caught off-guard and fell from the tree. It started to fly, but Therm kept the water steady and knocked it from the sky onto his lawn, where it lay stunned.

Therm stood over the bird and sprayed it again for good measure. He bent down to flick the parrot's head and it snipped his hand. Blood welled up around his knuckles. There was a rag in the shed. Also in the shed, the axe. By the time the bleeding stopped, he had convinced himself to chop the bird to pieces. He raised the axe. The parrot blinked a few times and made a feeble chirp. It kind of pouted like he'd seen his ex-wife pout. Therm couldn't follow through. He returned to the shed, noticed that his hand was bleeding again, and fired up the lawn mower. The bird raised its voice. Therm set the mower on course, closed his eyes, told himself, *This won't hurt a bit*, and pushed the machine forward.

Jakob Loomis was told to be home before dinner. That gave him plenty of time, he figured. He was meeting Tommy Tucker at the baseball diamond and the two of them were going to take Tommy's pellet gun to the pond and shoot tadpoles. When Jakob got to the baseball field, Tommy was already there, waiting in the dugout. He had a worried look on his face.

"Can't do it today, man," Tommy said.

"Why not?" Jakob asked.

"Mrs. Pratt called my mom and told her I cheated on our math test."

"Dumb Mrs. Fat," Jakob said.

"My mom grounded me. I told her I had to meet you and get the homework assignment, but I have to get back now. I brought the pellet gun if you want it."

The pond was located between two mounds of sand that Jakob had to walk over to get to the bank. The water was green and full of cattails and lily pads. Jakob spotted a tadpole, took aim, but decided not to fire. He couldn't figure out why he should. When Tommy had the pellet gun, he took careful aim, his tongue lolling out of his mouth, and fired. Nine out of ten times, the tadpole floated to the surface. This was impressive. But Jakob thought differently. There was no need to kill baby frogs, or any animal. He'd even set his pet parrot free because it seemed to complain about being caged all the time.

———

"Your hand's bleeding," the handcuffed man says. "Snakebite?"

"No. I must have cut it on the axe."

Therm lets his hand hang loosely and bleed. A thin rain begins to slant down over the men. The handcuffed man tilts his head back and lets the water cool his face. Droplets of moisture linger on his eyelashes and a fine layer of precipitation forms on his forehead and chin.

Therm glances down at his stained sneakers. When he tried to clean them with the hose, the blood had merely smeared. Therm had washed the pulpy remains of the parrot from the mower down to the fringe of the woods. A cloud of gnats hangs over the remains. In a wicked moment, Therm tries to imagine Madeline's face opening a package with the dead bird in it. Her jaw would drop and she'd cover her mouth with her ring-less hand. She'd probably shriek something dramatic like, *Oh, Christ, No!* and ask her cat-boyfriends what to do. They'd say call the police. Therm would send the package anonymously, of course, and he'd use gloves so that fingerprints weren't an issue. But there was a problem, Therm remembered. When the police asked Maddy about anything suspicious lately, she'd recall the odd message on her answering machine. The police would replay the tape with the recorded squawking and use a forensics team to determine that the pulpy mess had been a parrot and that the cawing on the tape had been a parrot. They'd trace the call somehow, arrest Therm, and he'd spend time in the slammer, humiliated. Better let the bird decompose in the rain and not make a big deal out of it.

"If you're not going to give me a drink of water, I think I'm going to move on," the handcuffed man says.

"You don't want to drink from that hose. The rain should be enough."

The handcuffed man licks his lips.

"As far as letting you just walk off," Therm says, "give me one good reason why I shouldn't call the police?"

The handcuffed man tries to look as relaxed as possible in handcuffs. He says, "Sometimes the police shouldn't be involved."

"Maybe so, but that doesn't explain the handcuffs."

"I'd rather not say."

"Then I better call the police."

"If you'll feel better about it, call them. But the reason for these cuffs has got nothing to do with them. It's more domestic."

"I'm listening."


Cole's Daddy was a snake handler and a preacher of the Gospel and of Jesus Christ the Savior, Our Lord. His Daddy told Cole he was born from a God-blessed serpent. Cole shared his crib with snakes, he learned to walk with snakes, and the first word out of his mouth was *hiss*. These things made Cole's Daddy proud. He took his son all over Texas to preach the faith and demonstrate with serpents that the Good Lord watched over the faithful. In a trance with a viper, Cole's Daddy got bit in the mouth. His lips and tongue turned rotten and made speaking nearly impossible. He tried to preach with just his hands, but nobody listened. So he turned to drinking. And he turned to his boy.

Cole really did like snakes. They were mostly quiet and friendly, and if there was any evil in them, he couldn't find it. After his Daddy got bit, Cole tried his best to keep the faith. He learned some sign language and tried to teach it to his father. His father just shook his fists and Cole got the message.

When the money ran out, Cole's Daddy figured he could use his son's natural snake abilities to earn them a living. He believed God owed him that, at least. There were a lot of tourists and nonbelievers who would be impressed if they saw his boy crawl out of a sleeping bag filled with rattlers and moccasins and such. With the little money he had saved, Cole's Daddy made flyers that read: *See the snakechild escape from a sleeping bag full of poison snakes!* The performance didn't draw a big crowd, but it brought in enough money to travel and to get Cole's Daddy cross-eyed drunk.

Cole found it tricky to crawl out of the sleeping bag filled with snakes because the snakes were packed so tightly together that they became irritated. He had to wait until they calmed down and then very carefully pull himself out to the crowd of anxious people and the applause. Each time he had to move a different way to keep from rolling over a snake's head. Once, after years of crawling out of the sleeping bag, during a Snake Roundup, just as Cole had pulled his head and shoulders out of the bag, a drunk said, *Bullshit, those snakes aren't poisonous,* and he threw his bottle. It wasn't a good throw and when it shattered in front of Cole a thin shard of glass struck the boy in the eye. The snakes hissed and snapped at one another as the crowd tried to decide what to do. The drunk thought he might have made a mistake. Everybody waited. Cole breathed lightly as his eye bled and the snakes settled. Finally, he crawled the rest of the way out.

The hospital couldn't save Cole's eye so they made him a glass one. Police went around arresting people for disorderly conduct and child neglect. Cole was sent to a foster home and

Cole's Daddy found refuge in the church where he tried his best to apologize through cheap religious cards on which he wrote, *Son, I'm so sorry, I'm really proud of you, God loves you and I do, too!* in sloppy cursive.

Cole finished growing up quietly. He made few friends and had trouble looking people in the eye. His closest relationship was with God. After Cole understood that he wasn't born from a serpent, he tried to figure out who his mother was. Through hospital records, and with reluctant help from his Daddy, Cole learned his mother lived in Florida and worked for a theme park there. Cole turned eighteen, took a bus to Central Florida, and paid for a ticket. Information directed him to the *Hop Along Trail!* His mother was a costumed, pink-furred rabbit who sang a happy song and hopped from foot to foot. Cole watched her in the thin crowd and munched on a candy apple. She was good at her job, a group of children clapped and danced to the song. The tune was catchy. Cole hummed along with the children. Nearby, a tall, young couple with a video camera glanced over disapprovingly. Cole realized he was out of place, all grown-up with candy apple on his mouth trying to have a moment with his mother in a sea of children. He blew a kiss and left.

An ad in the paper mentioned big bucks for capturing venomous snakes and selling them to pharmacies in order to make anti-venom. Cole aged, became a hunter. On good days, he'd gather a dozen serpents. Once in a while the law gave him trouble for trespassing while he was wrangling snakes in private property. He bought a trailer out in the country and tried to mind his own business. He had girlfriends here and there. He attended a Methodist church. His Daddy passed away Godless and broken. On the television, Cole learned about the missing boy and made a mental note to keep an eye out for him.

———

Out of the corner of his eye, Jakob caught sight of a frog at the waterline. It was a white frog. Jakob couldn't believe it. He had never seen a white frog and as far as he knew, they didn't exist. But here one was. Setting the gun aside, Jakob crept closer to the frog and dove for it. He missed, slid half into the water, getting his pant leg soaked, and leaned against the mound to wait for the frog to reappear. It popped up on the other side. Jakob stalked it more carefully and when he got close enough, he wiggled one hand out as a distraction and plunged his other hand in after the frog. This time Jakob was successful. He pulled it from the water by a long white leg and clutched it to his body. His heart pounded and he tried to catch his breath. *A white frog!* Tommy wasn't going to believe this. Jakob had to keep the frog to show Tommy tomorrow after school. The frog was slippery and he nearly dropped it as he climbed over the mounds and away from the pond. He'd leave the pellet gun there for now, find an old soda can or something to put it in, and show it off tomorrow. Then he'd set it free. It wasn't dinnertime yet, the sun still had some life in it. All he had to do was find a container.

"I've been seeing this woman named Samantha for a while, and the other day she says she wants to spice up our love-making," Cole says to Therm after a considerable pause in their conversation.

The rain turns to a wet mist. Cole leans his shoulder against the side of the house. Therm sets the axe between his legs.

"Of course, I don't know what this means," Cole continues. "She says the ways we've been doing it is how she's always done it and she wants to try bondage."

"Bondage?" Therm asks.

"That's what I said. I don't know about you, but I'm not exactly the most experienced rooster in the coop."

Therm nods. Maddy never mentioned bondage.

"So, I go over to her place around noon to see what she has in mind."

"She had handcuffs planned, huh?"

"Yes, and a blindfold. She cuffed me and called me a filthy bastard. I thought she meant it, but she explained this was role-playing and told me to wait in the *dungeon* while she freshened up. The dungeon was the bedroom, but I was supposed to use my imagination. I waited a long damned time sitting there on her bed. When you can't see and you don't know what's coming to you your mind starts thinking awful things."

"It does," Therm says, "it sure does."

"I tried to get out of the handcuffs but couldn't. I wondered where she got the handcuffs and where she put the key. Hell, I even started thinking that she was going to chop me up like you read about in papers. Lovers get chopped up for one reason or another."

"True," Therm agrees.

"Then I heard some shouting out in the front yard. There was another man's voice. This made me nervous, as you can imagine. I didn't know if she was going to bring some guy into this bondage experience or what."

"So what did you do?"

"I put my face into the bed and rubbed that blindfold off. Out the front window I saw Samantha arguing with this big guy, bigger than you, about something. Come to find out, it's her husband."

"She's married?"

Cole blows a low whistle.

"That's awful."

"I thought so, too. I looked for the handcuff key, but it wasn't in the bedroom. About the time that big boy comes busting in the front door, I manage to get out the back door and run for my life. I had to leave my car there. I imagine he had it impounded."

Therm rubs his fingers on the axe handle. After a moment he says, "You shouldn't have run."

"He probably would have given me a good whupping."

"Maybe you deserve one."

"Not in handcuffs."

"How long have you been cheating with her?"

"Oh, I don't know, a month."

"And you never thought to ask her if she was married?"

"It never came up."

"Couldn't you tell a man lived with her? Men's shaving cream in the bathroom, shoes under the bed, trophies?" Therm shifts the axe from hand to hand.

"Most of the time she came to my place. She didn't wear a ring."

"Of course she wouldn't wear her ring. Cheaters know better than that," Therm says.

"Well, whatever. I just hate being caught up in this mess. I'd like to go back and sort it out with this guy. He's probably rational enough. I'll apologize. Is that what you think I should do?"

"It won't be enough, but it will be a start. The major damage is done. Don't even think about seeing her again, though. How would you feel if your wife was bonding with some other man?"

"I've never been married."

"Yeah, well."

"But I didn't know she was married."

"Now you do."

"I'll talk to him."

Therm sucks on his teeth.

"I'll go right now. I just wish I didn't have these damned handcuffs on."


At approximately 3:15 p.m., Officer Ferris noted, a man in a blue Chevy Nova, 1986 or so, drove by with a busted taillight. Ferris had been instructed to stop any vehicles that drew suspicion and might possibly be carrying the missing boy. A busted taillight suggests a struggle; the boy could be in the trunk, tied down and helpless. Ferris flipped his lights on and pursued the blue Chevy Nova.

The afternoon was calm with heavy, low clouds above harboring rain. Since the boy disappeared, the weather had been somber. Ferris had tried to stay objective about the disappearance, he didn't want to rule out all the possibilities. The boy could have run off or fallen into a sinkhole or just gotten himself really lost. But Ferris had dismissed these considerations after combing the woods with the boy's mother a few nights ago. Ferris had been assigned to survey the woods with the mother while other officers worked deeper in the woods and the surrounding neighborhoods. After nightfall, the mother and Ferris followed their erratic flashlights around the soft sounds of crickets and distant shufflings. The first time the mother cried her son's name, Ferris had flinched. The immediate loudness of her pain-filled voice frightened him. The more she called out, the more serious the situation seemed. Ferris eventually yelled for the boy, too, as much to hear his own voice responding to hers as to hope for a feeble reply from the woods. By sunrise,

Ferris was spent and hoarse and convinced the boy had been nabbed. The mother's doomsday worry had seeped into him throughout the night. "A mother knows," she said, and Ferris knew better than to disagree.

The team of officers uncovered a pellet gun by the pond, and a dead frog in a paper bag near the old elementary school. Footprints were either trampled by the team or erased by the drizzle and mist. Now, though, with the weather keeping the ground soft, if the kidnapper made a move, there was a good chance they would find prints or tire tracks or something that spelled foul play.

The blue Chevy Nova signaled and pulled to the shoulder of the road. 3:18 p.m., Officer Ferris noted, and it's showtime. He exited his squad car, adjusted his belt, keeping his hand near his sidepiece, and approached the car. The perpetrator rolled his window down, stuck his head out, and said, "Is there a problem, officer?"

The perpetrator had stringy hair, sun-darkened skin, and a long chin. His eyes, Ferris determined, were shifty and cold.

"License and registration," Ferris demanded, keeping his eyes on the perpetrator's hands.

The man dug into his glove compartment. A Bible fell out, which seemed odd to Ferris. *Why would a man keep one in his glove box?* It didn't make sense. "You a man of the cloth?" Ferris questioned.

"No, sir, I'm not. There are some passages I like to read before I go to work."

The man handed Ferris the documents. The perpetrator's name was Cole Bateman. He had vision impairment and lived in a remote trailer park just over the county line. This guy fit the profile of a child molester, Ferris knew: late twenties, white, scrawny, a loner, overly religious, dirt under the fingernails; all typical. As Ferris returned the license, he heard a faint thud in the trunk.

"Out of the car," Ferris said, withdrawing his gun and pointing it in Cole's face.

"What?" Cole asked, recoiling.

"Out, now." Ferris flung the door open and Cole cautiously stepped onto the road.

"Hands on the hood."

Cole put his hands on the hood. Ferris yanked the perpetrator's arms behind his back and cuffed him.

"Stay put," Ferris said.

"What did I do?"

Ferris glared at the handcuffed man. "I'm going to find out just what you did."

It took Ferris a few moments to locate the trunk-release latch and his adrenaline made his hands fumble and his heart jump. He heard movement in the trunk again, no mistake about it. The trunk popped.

The perpetrator said, "I caught those on public property," and Ferris raised his gun again. He told Cole to shut up, pervert.

In the trunk was a large potato sack thrashing from side to side. Ferris holstered his gun and pulled the sack to the edge of the trunk. It was lighter than a boy should be. He was probably starving, poor thing. Ferris loosened the knot at the neck of the sack and opened it. A cottonmouth struck his wrist, released its fangs, and struck his hand in an instant. A pygmy rattler attached itself to a finger on his other hand. Ferris flung the sack back into the trunk and shook the pygmy rattler from his finger. He screamed some oaths, drew his gun, and shot at the sack of snakes.

Cole ran.

Ferris lifted his gun and fired at the retreating perpetrator. His shot missed badly. The man scurried off into the forest. There was only a moment of hesitation, and then Ferris was in pursuit. A copperhead escaped, slid across the asphalt, and buried itself in a pile of woody pulp.

Jakob wandered around the woods looking for litter. He found a battered trash bag and broken glass, but nothing he could keep the frog in. His old elementary school was not far from here, maybe a half-mile. The school had burned down after a fire started in the boiler room. The police said nobody was hurt, but the students believed the janitor had been trapped down in the basement and died. Tommy Tucker said that the teachers and parents didn't want the kids to know because the janitor's corpse had been burnt so badly it would give everyone nightmares to think about. Everyone thought about it anyway.

In a trash can on the playground Jakob found a paper bag that could hold the white frog. The school was nothing more than a pile of rubble with a few scorched half-walls tugging out of the ground. Firefighters had cleaned up the site and there were plans to reconstruct it in a few years.

The playground was undamaged. Jakob poked a few holes in the bag for the frog to breathe, set it near the jungle gym, and ran over to the merry-go-round. Jakob couldn't resist the merry-go-round. He grabbed the rusty green bars and grunted as he pushed it around, kicking up dirt. The merry-go-round squealed in protest, but as Jakob persisted and it gathered momentum, the noise stopped and with a final shove, he leapt up on it.

Jakob stood in the middle and tried to keep his balance without holding onto the bars. He loved the sensation of being dizzy; it was as if he were in a different world when he was spinning, a slower, dreamy world. He went around and around. Overhead, the high afternoon sky threw his shadow to the graveled ground. Jakob watched the image in front of him grow from kid-size to adult-size to giant-size. At its peak, Jakob raised his arms so that the shadow's fingers stretched nearly to the woods. And in an instant, as the merry-go-round rotated and he turned to face the sun, his shadow diminished to regular size and smaller until it disappeared altogether.

Blinded, Jakob could not see the shadow that had been pacing him rise up and out of the ruins of the school.

"I'd help you, but I'm no good at picking locks," Therm says, considering the handcuffs. "Besides, if you go to the husband restrained, you'll score sympathy points."

"Yeah, or he'll see what Samantha had in mind. He'll be forced to think of she and me getting it on in bondage." Cole thrusts his hips. The shackles jangle.

"Don't do that."

"Well. It'd be best if I returned with open arms. Plus, you might want me to have a closer look at that wound. If a snake bit you, we should do something about it."

"I told you it wasn't a snake, and I told you I don't pick locks."

"Well, I don't either. Do you know any locksmiths?"

"Man, I don't even know my neighbors."

"Maybe we could clip it with something from your woodshed?"

"I use that for the lawn mower and not much else."

"What about the axe?"

Therm lifts the axe and raises his eyebrows.

"I'll bet you could bust the chains in three swings, big boy like yourself."

"What if I miss?"

"I don't know, try not to. Take good aim. I'd do just about anything to have these off. You ever been handcuffed?"

When they were children Therm and his brother used to play Cowboys and Indians. Therm always ended up the restrained Indian, but he didn't mind. Those were toy handcuffs made from plastic and when Therm pulled hard they'd open enough to slide free. When Therm tried to run away, his brother shot him up with cap guns.

"Sure," Therm says to Cole, "I've been cuffed before."

"You know, then, the Good Lord never intended to keep a man locked like this," Cole says, shaking his arms. "How am I supposed to pray with my arms behind my back?"

Therm doesn't pray, but he thinks about it sometimes.

"I've learned my lesson," Cole says. "My wrists feel like they've been rubbed over with sandpaper."

"They're red."

"I'll go kneel by that stump, stretch the chain back as far as it will go, and let you have a whack at it. Then I'll go apologize and take myself out of Samantha and her husband's relationship for good. Maybe they can get counseling and patch things up."

"Counseling could work if they're both willing to try," Therm agrees. "It isn't a bad idea."


3:53 p.m., Ferris notes, and he is in trouble. The snakebite at his wrist has quickly pumped poison into his bloodstream. According to the police handbook, which Ferris knows by memory, you aren't supposed to try and suck the poison out of a snakebite, but he tries anyway. With a piece of his shirt, he makes a tourniquet around his arm. He fears this is too late. He has gotten himself lost in the woods and regrets his hasty decision to pursue the perpetrator. The handbook never mentioned chasing a suspected child molester into the woods after you've been bit repeatedly by deadly snakes. The handbook mentioned backup. *So*, Ferris rationalizes, *I've made a mistake.* His right hand looks like an eggplant and the damaged finger on his left hand is paralyzed and swollen. Breathing is difficult. It had rained around 3:45 p.m. and then it stopped; now there is mist. Ferris is pretty sure he has passed that pepper tree three times.

In a small clearing, Ferris notices footprints that are smaller than his own. They lead around a bramble bush and farther into the forest. Unsteadily, Ferris follows.

4:10 p.m., and Ferris is on his hands and knees, gasping for breath and crawling from one footprint to the next. He can no longer feel the right side of his body and his vision has blurred. Still, he struggles forward, not yet ready to die.

The footprints stop. Ferris props himself on his elbows where the woods end and the grass of someone's backyard begins. In the yard, a man lifts an axe and hesitates. Ferris only sees the back of a small person kneeling, arms behind him, before the executioner. He thinks of the missing boy. With his left hand, Ferris draws his gun, a last surge of energy carries his shaking arm up, and he fires. The axe falls.

Therm feels a burning in his chest as he heaves forward and drives the axe hard into the handcuffed man's wrist. He falls to his knees beside Cole and tries to find some explanation in the man's face.

The bite of steel in Cole's wrist doesn't hurt at first. He can't believe the idiot missed. He was so close to freedom. But the pain comes when he tries to move his hand and feels that it is mostly detached from his arm. The warm flow of his blood down his backside drains him quicker than he thinks it should, and Cole finds he cannot stand up or stop the bleeding.

Ferris congratulates himself for doing the right thing. The police handbook, as he recalls, says, in Chapter Three: *At all costs protect the victim.* Or maybe it was, *On most occasions look out for the good guy.* Something like that. No matter. He rests his face in the grass. He'd like to check his watch to note the time of rescue but he doesn't have the energy to lift his poisoned arm.

Therm fingers the hole in his chest and recalls Cowboys and Indians. The wound is perfectly circular and seems fake peeking out from his torn shirt. He figures he'll play dead for a while. He falls forward and hides his face in the lawn.

Cole collapses, chin first. He tugs at the handcuffs weakly, but his hand won't snap off. There's still enough bone to keep him locked.

The men take in the scent of the earth. Each locates a memory from when he was a child playing in the freshly cut grass, invincible and alive. They remember how easy it was to be a boy.

# STILL LIFE

The Adopt-a-Railroad program didn't seem like such a bad idea at first. Mr. Ralph, the art teacher, championed it. So much trash collects along the tracks, with the constant whoosh of the locomotives sucking it in and huffing it back out. Why not get the kids out of the classroom and into the world? Life's dirty, boys and girls.

"And look at the precedents," Mr. Ralph said to the PTA. "Adopt-a-Highway, Adopt-a-Beach, Adopt-a-Tree, Adopt-a-Grandparent, Adopt-a-Cemetery. This stuff's gold on a college résumé."

Mr. Ralph had consulted the train schedule. There was a perfect window during fourth period. Parents and teachers agreed to give it a try. After all, summer break was around the corner, and everyone was getting antsy for the end.

Everett Zurn had grown accustomed to his station at Strand High. He wasn't an athlete or an anarchist. He had never given the counselor any reason to include his name on the "At Risk" list. He came from a modest family: his mother was a cashier at the Handi-Mart, and his father worked two-week stints in the coal mines of Pennsylvania and West Virginia. The boy was often left alone, but he did not mind it. He was not smart and was not stupid, did not really try or rebel—just another of the vast minority of through-the-crack slippers.

Once he finished high school, he'd become a miner. It's what Zurn men did. He was mostly fine with this. It didn't matter that teachers overlooked him; he'd be underground soon enough. All the same, Everett sometimes felt the future waiting for him pressing down, making it hard to breathe. And the only time this pressure let up was in art class.

Everett had always liked to draw. It was a way to excavate what was in his head and pass time. His work had gone through many phases. Currently, he was into caricatures. He could portray all of his teachers and most of his classmates.

His art teacher, Mr. Ralph, was one of his favorite subjects. The thinning hair, the middle-aged belly and the moustache. But it was also the way Mr. Ralph carried himself, like he didn't belong in Strand. He was the only teacher who hadn't grown up in their small town, and Everett often found himself examining the man's face, trying to capture that difference.

Today Mr. Ralph was explaining that night's self-portrait homework assignment, and Everett was trying hard to concentrate.

"In order to *capture* your essence," Mr. Ralph said, "you have to *find* yourself." When Mr. Ralph talked, he had a habit of pacing and would occasionally roll his shoulders back as if he were trying to rid himself of a heavy weight. "At your age, I don't expect you to really know who you are. You won't be graded on that. I do, however, encourage you to examine what's *beneath* your skin. Find a mirror and study your face. Breathe life into it. When I look at your lips, I expect them to whisper a secret."

Everett wasn't sure what this meant. After class, he approached Mr. Ralph for clarification.

Mr. Ralph was busy cleaning up the work stations. "Just surprise me," he said. "Surprise yourself."

"I'll try," Everett said. He picked at his fingernails before asking, "Are you going to do one?"

Mr. Ralph set the brown paper towel roll aside and considered his student. He could not pinpoint the kid's name. He put a hand to his chin and tried to gauge the boy's sincerity. These days it was hard to tell when his chain was being yanked. "Why would I do one? I'm the teacher."

"You're an artist too, right?"

"It's been a long time since anyone called me that," Mr. Ralph said sarcastically, as if speaking to somebody else. "But you're right, I am. I'll give it a try."

At home, Everett slipped into the guest bathroom downstairs and studied himself. There were tiny roosters dotting the yellow wallpaper behind him. It would be easy to draw a cartoonish version of himself, but that wasn't the assignment. Outside, he slumped into a green plastic chair on the front porch in the dwindling evening. He hid inside his brown hoodie. His father's portable Coleman grill reclined next to Everett, and the distorted image staring back resembled the Grim Reaper. He drew a grinning skull peeping out of the hood. Mr. Ralph had mentioned that the face should come alive. So Everett added flesh to the mouth and flushed the cheeks. Wheat-colored hair draped across his forehead. He had always been good at noses. The eyes, though, were difficult. Sometimes they were green and sometimes gray, but they were always darting and impossible to pin down. He tried and tried. Then, fortunately, it was night. Life somehow felt more natural in the absence of light. Without thinking about it, he rummaged through the grill and

rubbed a charcoal briquette lightly over his portrait. He en-
titled it, *Me, In the Dark.*


Before he became a teacher, Mr. Ralph had been a different
man. He was an artist. His work appeared in galleries in New
Haven. He once sold a neo-impressionistic painting for ten
thousand dollars. He attended parties hosted by noted remod-
ernists. He was a valued member of a scene that was on the
cusp of a new movement that never happened. Instead, figura-
tive painting caught fire in London. Mr. Ralph declared it a
fad, but his compatriots weren't so sure. They eschewed con-
ceptual art and flew to London.

Mr. Ralph kept at it in Connecticut, living from painting
to painting in a studio by the river until he couldn't support
himself any longer. Then he put two and two together and
joined the ranks of dreamers who acquire teaching certificates
and skulk into classrooms, seduced by the promise of summers
off. He settled in a small, blue-collar town in central Pennsylvania, replacing a beloved art teacher who had gone on a cruise
and never returned. The job at Strand High was all right. But
Mr. Ralph's appreciation for his new life had less to do with
inspiring students and free summers than it did with Millie
Baumgartner.

Millie was a choreographer who occasionally helped direct
the high school dance team. One cloudy afternoon after the
students had trudged off and Millie was cleaning up her desig-
nated area in the gymnasium, Mr. Ralph made his move. He
slipped a CD into the portable player, waited for "I've Got
You Under My Skin" to come on, and said, "May I have this
dance?"

Millie didn't ordinarily go for corny. But she was from Strand and turning into a townie in spite of herself. At least this man, with his neatly mustached smile, was from someplace else. She took his quivering hand. He wasn't half-bad. He didn't shuffle his feet or step on hers.

So began the relationship. Mr. Ralph took her back to his modest apartment by the railroad tracks and showed her his terrific rooftop balcony. When he wasn't in the classroom, he was on the roof painting cloudscapes. Millie reclined in a lounge chair with a mojito. She would lazily tell Mr. Ralph what she saw in the clouds—a lion, a petunia, a bridge, a carrot, a leprechaun—and Mr. Ralph would make bold, confident brushstrokes. She started calling him Mr. Raphael. They hardly noticed the trains hustling by. Those were the Cumulonimbus Days. After sunset, they'd dance on the balcony and make love on a blow-up mattress under the stars. The wind would pick up, and away they'd fly.


Considering the crooked, dopey faces Everett saw branded with *A*s that were handed back to his peers, he was crestfallen when Mr. Ralph returned his self-portrait marked with a *D*. Even the kid he spied scribbling on a piece of loose-leaf in the bathroom minutes before class—an oblong balloon head with a squiggly line for a mouth and unfinished stars for eyes—got a *B*.

When Everett approached Mr. Ralph after class to talk about the grade, Mr. Ralph shooed him away. He had tomorrow—Adopt-a-Railroad Day—to plan. As for his teacher's self-portrait, Mr. Ralph conveniently forgot to bring it in. It would be easy enough, Everett thought, to capture Mr. Ralph's essence. Just draw a steaming pile of manure and dot it with a swarm of flies.

Everett stewed through the afternoon. Walking home from school along the tracks, the boy could not suppress the prickle of rage clawing up his spine. He stepped quickly from one railroad tie to the next. His portrait was not a masterpiece, of course, but it was better than a *D*. He considered wadding it up and tossing it into the brush. Let Mr. Ralph clean it up with the rest of the trash tomorrow.

That's when Everett spotted the deer carcass in a ditch beside a section of railroad tracks. It was a young buck. The haunches had been mashed where it was likely swiped by a car on the nearby county road. A thin antler was snapped. The buck's gray tongue lolled in the grass.

If he were still a kid, Everett would have found a stick and prodded the gelatinous eyes. Or hurried home to his father, who might have carved it up for the grill if the meat had not spoiled. Now he held his elbow in his hand and saw the way the animal's body shone in the light. He thought about how he would draw it, in charcoal and pencil. How he would shade and texture so that the buck seemed alive. So alive he could imagine it speaking. He contemplated what came next for its body: a meal for possum and turkey vultures, an incubator of maggots, rot and decay.

*I could be something more*, the dead deer said.

Everett squinted at the carrion in the wavering afternoon balm. "Like what?"

*A lesson. An expression. A way out. You adopt me, I adopt you.*

At first, this didn't make sense to Everett—a coy riddle conjured from a dead deer.

And then it did.


The next day, the eleventh-graders piled onto the bus for the short trip to the mile-long stretch of railroad they'd adopted.

Everett sat quietly in the back row with his rowdy peers. He was in the same brown hoodie he wore every day. That morning he'd said goodbye to his parents as they left to visit his aunt in the city. Then he'd opened his backpack and slipped in an extra set of clothes, a blanket, and his sketchbook.

When they arrived, Mrs. Kenard, the bus driver, stayed on the bus. She would honk the horn at precisely 1:45 so the kids could climb back on and return to school by fifth period. This gave them plenty of time. The next train wouldn't come through until 3:15.

As the students filed off the bus, Mr. Ralph handed each one a pair of rubber gloves and a garbage bag. Everett kept his hood drawn, accepting the materials but refusing to make eye contact with Mr. Ralph.

"All right, everyone," Mr. Ralph said, "let's pair up and get to work."

Everett was already edging away from the crowd. The rest of the students radiated apathy as they walked the rails, listless, ignoring candy wrappers, soda cans, scraps of newspaper, cigarette butts, doll parts.

"Heads down, boys and girls," Mr. Ralph said. "Keep your heads down!" He had two bags full in no time. It felt good to stay busy and not think about Millie, but it was also hard, since technically Adopt-a-Railroad was for her. Her father, a man Millie had never introduced Mr. Ralph to, used to be a conductor, and his recent passing had made her nostalgic for the good old days of comforting smoke plumes and happy whistles, the chug-a-chug-a-choo-choo. Mr. Ralph had thought that getting out and doing something positive might help her heal.

"You could chaperone," he suggested one evening on his rooftop. "Maybe we could even create a scholarship in his name."

"When I was a kid, my father was gone all the time. Mom and I were always waiting for him to come home." Millie lipped a flask of tequila. "I think it made us love him stronger."

"Fundraiser?" Mr. Ralph offered, adding a dab of burnt sienna to the troposphere.

In hindsight, Mr. Ralph should have seen the storm brewing. Millie visited infrequently in the weeks following the funeral. All he had to do was look at his canvas, at the black, threatening clouds he'd been producing. Those were Cirrus Days, and darkening. Or, on the occasions when Millie was around, he could have paid closer attention to her descriptions of the clouds—a knife, a vampire, a headstone, handcuffs, a highway.

Out of the blue, Millie took a bus to Albuquerque to be with a woman she'd met online named Spirit who made dream weavers for a living. Mr. Ralph told himself this was part of the grieving process; she needed some kind of awakening in the desert. Afterwards, she'd return. It was easy math: Her Being Gone + Him Being Here Waiting = Stronger Love Forever.

Millie didn't return Mr. Ralph's calls. One time she texted him: *Believe what you want. If it's easier for you to think I'm dead, think it. That's how I'll be thinking of you.*

The message stung, of course. Mr. Ralph tried not to take it personally. For weeks, then months (as the PTA deliberated over his Adopt-a-Railroad program), Mr. Ralph prepared his face to look stern-yet-welcoming when she walked back through the door. Sinatra was cued and waiting on his portable CD player. She'd be impressed at the success of the Adopt-a-Railroad initiative. They'd patch things up. If she wanted, he'd even move out West.

Mr. Ralph was contemplating what clouds would look like cresting desert mountains when Mrs. Kenard blew the bus horn. All aboard. Loose sacks of garbage occupied the last few rows. Back at school, there was still enough time to wash up before fifth period. Some good got done, Mr. Ralph thought, gliding down the hall. It was not until midway through the final period that he was called into the principal's office and interrogated regarding the whereabouts of Everett Zurn.


Everett moved down the tracks at a steady pace, walking in the shadow of the forest. He had looked back only once. Mr. Ralph had been stooping over a puddle of mud to fetch a broken kite, his pants hiked up so everyone could see that his socks were different shades of beige. The boy had turned away, certain that his absence would not be noticed.

This business of cleaning trash off the tracks was stupid, Everett knew. His house was right on top of the railroad. His first word was *twain*. He learned to count by watching locomotives pass and learned to read by sounding out the names on the sides of boxcars: Union Pacific, Great Northern, Hormel. Trains were gritty and loud and indifferent. Folks born along the rail understood this. Inside the house, you got used to the dishes clamoring, drowned-out *Days of Our Lives*, shadows racing across the living room wall, hearts still clutching and pumping in time with the machines long after they had passed. Nobody slept deeply, and just when your dreams started getting good, Amtrak rumbled by to remind you where you were. Lying in bed at night, Everett alternated between hating and envying the slumbering passengers. They were not from here, and they were not stuck here. They were just moving through.

He found the deer waiting for him right where he left it. Gloves still on, he dragged the thing with difficulty out of the ditch and onto the tracks where the rail bent around a copse of fir. The conductor would not have enough time to stop or even really see what he was pulverizing: a dead deer in a brown hoodie lying in still life repose.

*You sure about this?* the buck asked.

"I am." The boy took in rapid gulps of air.

*Hey, you know, I was thinking. Maybe you could curl up next to me—*

"No."

*Just a thought.* The deer was growing stiff. He was running out of time. *Police will ask where you've been.*

"Got turned around. Thought Mr. Ralph would come find me. Spent the afternoon lost in the woods. Finally managed to find my way back to the tracks. I'll give them this look." Everett made his practiced, sorry-but-it's-not-my-fault face, which involved parted lips, arched eyebrows, and wide, watery eyes.

*Needs work.*

Everett stripped down to his underwear and socks. He stuffed the deer's forelegs into the arm holes of his sweatshirt. He stretched the hood over what was left of the antlers.

*You'll get suspended.*

"Doubtful," Everett said, jamming hind hoofs into his jeans. "More likely Mr. Ralph will get canned."

*That what we're after?*

Everett caught a whiff of his mucky gloves as he wiped away a bead of sweat from the bridge of his nose. He turned away, choking down bile. "Damn, dude."

*What do you expect?*

The pants rode low on the buck's backside. Everett peeled off the gloves, keeping them at arm's length.

*How are you going to explain your clothes on me?*

"I don't know. Maybe you're an art project."

*And how did I get on the tracks?*

"Beats me." The boy fetched his change of clothes from his backpack. "I guess you weren't all-the-way dead."

*Someone might get hurt.*

"You can't derail a train."

*What about me? Are you sure I can't feel pain? You know, it's not too late—*

Everett ignored the deer as he scrambled up a small ridge out of earshot where he could wait for the 3:15 to arrive. He once saw his neighbor's deaf cat get hammered. There had been nothing left of Beethoven except a brief blood plume and a light sprinkle of fur.

The collision was different with the buck. On impact, the body split open and the insides splattered the forest scruff in a gory tableau that took his breath away. It was beautiful and sickening, and Everett felt the image worming into the back of his mind, where it would take up permanent residence.

By the time the train's brakes stopped screaming, the boy was gone.


The PTA called an emergency meeting. Not everyone could attend, but everyone tried. Parents gave their children an extra squeeze before leaving home. Marsha Tibble made cookies on short notice. Finn McGill feverishly wiped down his combover and trembled with outrage. The Warners sympathetically took smoke breaks. Mr. Darden, the English teacher, confessed that he thought Adopt-a-Railroad was a spectacularly poor idea.

"Hank's an all right guy," Mr. Darden said. "A bit aloof. And we definitely have a different artistic aesthetic."

Several faculty members managed brittle chuckles.

"Let's just say I didn't cast my vote in favor of the Adopt-a-Railroad proposal," Mr. Darden continued. "Not that I'm

fault-finding here. I know several of you in this room acqui-
esced on principle. Who can blame you? My point, and correct
me if I'm wrong, Monty, is that history teaches us that the
greatest danger comes from the man who concocts the plan."

Mrs. Drable, Mr. Penaski, Mrs. Youngblood, Mr. Finch,
and Mrs. Krunkle nodded in agreement.

"Has anyone spoken to Mr. and Mrs. Zurn?" asked Mrs.
Sparkle, the librarian.

"No one's been able to reach them yet," Donnie Sapolo
breathed. "We've left messages."

"If only Mr. Lundgrin had never gone on that cruise," muttered Cathy Grayson.

"Our children are not the chain gang," shouted Finn McGill.

Mrs. Jermito, the biology teacher, scanned the crowd.
"Where the hell is Mr. Ralph?"


Mr. Ralph arrived at the scene of the accident in a haze of con-
fusion. Authorities were questioning the distraught conductor,
who pulled his cap down over his eyes and crushed his hands
into his pockets. It was pretty easy to arrange the pieces of this
particular puzzle. They had found blood-drenched swaths of
Everett's hoodie clinging to the underside of leaves on low-
hanging branches. A few sizeable chunks of flesh had been sent
to the lab in order to confirm it was the boy. But locals weren't
waiting for the results. Word had already ricocheted through
town: *Everett Zurn was killed by a train.*

The town was asking, *Who's responsible?*

*Millie?* Mr. Ralph offered meekly, to himself.

Standing near the tracks and bathed in the swirling police
lights, Mr. Ralph tried to battle back a breakdown. He found
himself drifting away from his body. It took all his effort to re-

main clearheaded under a barrage of questions from authorities. He gave short, clipped answers and watched in horror as the police tape unraveled around stained tree trunks. They used up two rolls. He excused himself to get discreetly sick by his car.

Back home now, lying on the mostly deflated air mattress, he stared at the cloud-knitted sky and contemplated calling Millie. Just hearing her voice would be a comfort. Instead, what he heard was a distant train. He was surprised how quickly the world was returning to normal. What he wouldn't give to be aboard. At the sound of the locomotive's whistle, he couldn't help picturing the Zurn boy on the tracks with his plastic bag of trash, the gruesome moment of impact. Had the boy done this on purpose? Mr. Ralph tried to remember if there were any signs he'd overlooked. Was it the Zurn kid who blew off the self-portrait assignment? Best to let professionals sort through these things. Besides, nobody said anything about a note. This was just a tragic accident. It was nobody's fault. His heart went out. He knew he needed to do something. Boxcar after boxcar thumped by on the tracks below, the longest train in the world. Mr. Ralph couldn't see them from the air mattress, but he could feel them tugging him to his feet.

Everett's father had introduced the boy to the cave when he was thirteen. The entrance was tucked into an old coal hollow not far from the train tracks and easy to miss. When he was young, the father used to explore it, too. He'd even taken Everett's mother there when they were dating.

Most of the tunnels off the antechamber had collapsed, but there were still mysteries to uncover if you were willing to get dirty. Everett's father demonstrated how to shimmy headfirst on your back through spaces too tight to breathe deeply while holding a flashlight in his mouth. He explained how to count your way out of a claustrophobic panic. And on the other side of one particular tunnel, his father guided Everett to an opening with room enough to stand. Around an underground pool was another tunnel large enough to crawl through on hands and knees. At thirteen, Everett eagerly followed. The tunnel ended in a sinkhole. Everett's father switched off the flashlight and told his son to close his eyes, count to ten, and look up. The boy did. Twenty yards above, through an opening the size of a manhole, Everett could see stars even though it was the middle of the day.

As he grew older, Everett showed a few kids the cave. They'd spray paint the walls with graffiti. Over time the cave became a place for weekend parties, to which Everett was not always invited. Most people didn't have the guts to push through the tight spot to the interior alcove. But one time Everett managed to convince a girl, Jamie, to follow him. He told her there was a surprise on the other side—meaning the sinkhole and the stars in the daylight. He'd wanted to see the awe in her face before explaining scattered light and how the mystery was possible; he'd uncovered the reason in the school library. When they emerged into the small chamber with the underground pool, Jamie said, "Wait, what's that?" She had taken Everett's hand and circled the flashlight around the lair. At the time, Everett was in a monster phase.

"You draw these?" Jamie had asked.

"This isn't what I wanted you to see," Everett had said too loudly. His voice echoed off the zombies, werewolves, troglodytes, and demons he'd chalked onto the walls.

Jamie backed away, spooked. "I think I should leave," she'd said, and Everett had handed her the flashlight.

Today the drawings looked faded. After relieving himself in the underground pool, Everett ducked through the tunnel to the sinkhole, where he would kill time until nightfall. Let the rest of the world be damned without him. He spread out the blanket he'd brought, then folded his arms behind his head and gazed up the hole. Today the stars were covered by clouds.

He dug out his sketchbook and started to draw. First, he outlined the deer as he first found it, the way the light fell across the animal's fur, the way it seemed so alive. Then he started remembering all the ways the deer had come to pieces. The line of gore and blood along the tracks. For a moment, he imagined himself taken with it, his own body ground down by the train, and with each stroke of the pencil, Everett pushed harder into the paper until it left a mark on the page below.


Mr. Ralph consulted the phone book. The Zurns were the last name listed. As it turned out, they lived less than a mile from his apartment. On the walk over, dread squeezing his chest, he prepared what he would say: *I don't pretend to know how you're feeling and I know it isn't much, but I want to offer you my deepest condolences from the bottom of my heart.* Or, *From the bottom of my heart, I offer you my deepest condolences, even though I couldn't possibly understand the pain you must be going through right now. If you'd like to punch me in the face, I don't blame you. My plan was to help someone heal, to get over the loss of her father, which didn't work, and now I've caused more heartache. I am not a father, myself. Maybe someday, if I find the right woman. But of course this isn't about me. Your son was a wonderful boy, a joy in the classroom. You should be proud. Not that I'm suggesting how you should or should not feel.*

Much to Mr. Ralph's relief, the Zurns were not home. He rang the buzzer again, just to be sure. The porch light cast a dull glow on a tilting Coleman grill and a plastic chair. He wasn't sure what to do now. Leave a note? He didn't have a pen or paper. Besides, how do you say you're sorry in a letter? What he'd really like to do is retreat to his apartment, hop in the car, and go. He could be in Albuquerque in two days, three days tops. Or jet to England, if his passport wasn't expired.

Mr. Ralph slumped into the chair, lowered his head between his knees, and tried to swallow his thoughts. It was all his fault—the Zurn boy, Millie leaving, his own failed career. A train passed, right behind the boy's house, and shook the wooden porch. Mr. Ralph clutched the arms of the plastic chair and waited for the cars to pass, watching his reflection, distorted in the hood of the grill.


Outside, it was getting dark. Everett missed his hoodie. He heard a train whistle up ahead. Maybe nobody had noticed he was gone after all. That seemed fitting. Perhaps, once the train stopped, the conductor stuck his head out the window, convinced himself it was only a stray mutt, and kept going. Just left the mess behind. That's what he would have done.

When he got to the tracks, Everett had to wait for a train to pass before he could proceed. It was moving slowly enough that he could hop it: run alongside an open boxcar, grab the cool metal handle, and swing himself up. He had done it before, joyrides to the edge of town. One time his pal Mark decided to keep going. The police found him three days later, two states away, sleeping in an empty cattle car. It turned out Mark was running away because his father had found a job in

Lexington and they were moving. Running away because you were moving didn't make any sense to Everett.

After the curtain of train slid past, Everett saw the webbing of police tape strung around the trees like garland. In places it was torn in ribbons from the force of passing trains. There was a small white cross on the far embankment. He cautiously approached and stood before it, just as the dead buck's spirit rose out of the woods, majestic, complete, glowing. It floated to the boy's side.

"Damn, they're quick." Everett nudged the cross with his sneaker.

*What did you expect?*

"I don't know. Not this. Did it hurt?"

*Not really.*

"Sorry."

*You got want you wanted.*

"What's that?"

The dead buck shrugged and pawed the ground.

"Guess I should get back."

*Mom and Dad will be home soon. Maybe they already heard. They'll be sick to death.*

Everett yanked the cross from the soft earth and held it at arm's length.

*People care that you're gone.*

"No, they don't." He tossed the cross into the gravel. "This good Christian guilt shit makes me tired."

The phantom deer turned away from him. *Then you better wake up.*


When he heard footsteps on the walkway, Mr. Ralph popped out of the chair and blurted, "I'm so sorry—"

Everett froze. "Mr. Ralph?"

At first, Mr. Ralph didn't recognize the kid. Even when he did, it took a few moments to process. He lurched forward, caught himself at the last second, and stammered, "Is that you?"

It took every ounce of discipline in Everett's body to keep from bolting.

"I thought you were dead." Mr. Ralph blinked rapidly. There was a ringing in his ears. He stared in disbelief.

"It was a deer," the boy said quietly. "I found it next to the tracks."

"What?" Mr. Ralph tried to stop the ringing by rolling his shoulders. "Do you have any idea what you've put me through? What you've put everyone through?"

Everett took a small step backwards. He felt the familiar prickle of anger inching along his back. "You don't belong here."

Mr. Ralph swallowed something enormous that had been accumulating in his throat, and this somehow made him dizzy. "I'm going to sit down now. Please don't go."

Everett relaxed for a moment. His teacher's complexion was pale in the porch light reflecting off the grill. His face stretched gaunt.

"This is where I live."

"I know. I checked the phone book. I'm not far away."

In the quiet, they both heard a moth feverishly colliding against the porch light globe. Bits of powder fluttered from the wings. Slumped on the porch, Mr. Ralph seemed like a different man from Everett's caricatures. Even his moustache seemed to be drooping. Everett knew that he had done this. But it didn't make him feel any better.

"I guess you didn't do your self-portrait yet?" the boy asked.

"Self-portrait?"

"The homework assignment. You said you were going to do it."

"Oh, right. I haven't had time."

The boy took a tentative step closer. "Why'd you give me a *D*?"

Mr. Ralph sat up straight. "Is this about your grade?"

"I drew my face first and then rubbed it out."

"I didn't know that." Mr. Ralph studied the boy. Something, for sure, was circulating behind the kid's gray-green eyes. He turned his face to the sky, as if expecting to see clouds overhead. But it was dark, and the sky was dark too.

Using the arms of the chair for support, Mr. Ralph found his feet. "You still have it?"

Everett did. It was waiting in the backpack. "You can see me underneath the charcoal." The boy held out his assignment.

Mr. Ralph noticed that his hands were shaking as he took the portrait. He tilted the paper into the light and tried to steady himself. He wasn't sure what the hell was going on, and right now that didn't matter. He knew a bullet had been dodged. Here stood an opportunity to start anew. He could be a different man, a different artist, a different teacher. He had reinvented himself before. He'd start by getting over Millie. She was not coming back. No more painting cloudscapes. He would imagine a handsome, confident, capable version of himself and then sketch it—a self-portrait that he could grow into. Maybe shave the moustache. He'd publicly admit Adopt-a-Railroad was a horrendous idea, and, if necessary, he'd grovel to keep his job. He'd commit himself to the kids. In fact, he'd stop thinking of them as kids, but rather as students. Mr. Ralph could feel the boy's expectant eyes upon him.

"Well, I'll be damned, Everett," Mr. Ralph said, squinting into the mess, determined to see what he'd been missing. "You're right there."

# EVERYDAY MURDERS

Smoke remains weeks after the wildfire is contained. It hovers in the singed pine forest like an apparition and when rain gradually arrives, the recalcitrant southern ground sizzles.

Over 30,000 mostly-wooded acres in northeastern South Carolina were razed. Trees weren't the only victims. An Exxon exploded. The Fish Shack fried. Crops combusted. Meaningful golf courses were torched. The bog boiled creatures alive, concocting a moribund gumbo. Some birds couldn't climb high enough. The Golden Gardens retirement community was incinerated. Baffled, elderly residents were bussed to different homes across the state and into North Carolina. Orderlies did their best to keep friends and family together during the uprooting.

On the bright side, nobody knows of any human loss. This consolation allows people to clap each other on the back. It is a bit of solace in the aftermath of one-hundred feet waves of flame. In that space of calm come the questions. How in hell did it happen? Lots of ways, it could have: A cigarette tossed into the pine straw catches…a fool fails to observe his rusted-over tin garbage can heaped with leaves…an eager Cub Scout leader rubs two sticks together too fervently…teenagers with bad aim in a bottle rocket battle...a spouse eliminates incriminating bed sheets...

There are accidents and then there are conflagrations of the human heart. Reasons are drifting embers in a stiff wind. One of them turned the house to ashes.


Before the fire, up north, the first sign of life creeps out of the thawing ground. A tuft of weeds pushes into the early light. From his hideout in the attic and through the slatted window Grumman bears witness. Winter is winding down. Soon, the snowbirds will return.

The young man chose this two story house at the dead end with the brick façade and the frozen maple he used to shimmy and then shake onto the roof and through the dormer window into the attic—a space nobody wires for security—but he could have chosen any number of other houses. This neighborhood is unremarkable. The area is one of many northeastern regions populated by retirees who can afford to jump into and out of their lives with the changing season by occupying second homes. *The thing to do now*, Grumman realizes as he narrows his gaze at one splitting bud nestled up against the bare branch, *is trudge south.*

Grumman doesn't have much. The goal is to not need anything. The upstairs of the house is without a motion detector and he has been free to roam through the empty rooms. Sometimes he uses the rowing machine in the exercise room. He found a hand-held computerized chess game in the study and is getting better at it. Skims paperbacks. Sleeps in the guest room. Once in a while he takes a bath. When he arrived in early January he brought a duffel bag stuffed with boxes of cereal. He loves those fruity O's. He knows how to ration. He can slink around without ever passing in front of a window. He has memorized the sounds of the house and can predict when the heat will kick on. The owners set the temperature to fifty-eight, warm enough to keep the pipes from freezing. The phone nearly never rings. When it does (usually a solicitor or an accidental fax) the chipper voice on the answering machine lets the caller know that, "We're not here right now. Leave us a message and we'll get back to you when it's warmer!" Grumman always flinches when he hears the recording of the man's voice—it is not unlike his grandfather's—and chastises the owner, *May as well send thieves invitations.* These people are lucky to have Grumman watching over everything while they're away.

But spring is not far off. The fruity O's are nearly gone. Batteries are dead. The fair, even-keeled, cross-legged stupor he has maintained for most of the hours in the day will have to pause. Grumman's pretty satisfied with how deeply into himself he delved. He is getting better at drifting away.

Grumman cleans the house. All of the trinkets that he put into drawers on day one he rearranges. He'll leave the place cleaner than he found it. He shoulders the duffel and flits down the tree. This is the first time he has been outside in three months and his bones eagerly take to the fresh air. He crunches over the last remnants of snow and slides on a pair of thin, brown, driving gloves he lifted some time ago.

Up the street a man starts his car, a Cadillac, and leaves it running in the driveway to warm up before work.


Diblasio Weems slowly wraps his mouth around the word *entrepreneur.* He likes the taste of it. It is a label that has never been attributed to him before now. Names he has heard before: The Great White Whale, Blubbersaurus, Gigantahamster, Chief Stung-by-Bees. Sticks and stones, Diblasio knows. He is his own man now. Actually, he has created several identities online: Diablo, Blaze, WeeMonster, MrDiabolic.

"Entrepreneur," Diblasio says slowly to the potted cactus he's named Dave which sits upon his flimsy computer desk. The *Web Business Today* article, for which he was interviewed, has just been posted. Flabby arms folded over his robust gut, Diblasio bounces vigorously up and down on his meek swivel chair. He shakes the upstairs studio apartment around. When he throws his weight into it Diblasio can rotate a half-dozen times or more. He lifts his legs so that his toes touch the minifridge tucked under his desk and then the boxes of jerseys he's got stacked around the room. Beneath him china in the cabinet timidly clamors.

"Entreprefuckingneur, motherfuckers," he hollers, then his heart gives out—a soggy pop—and he completes two strong revolutions in his chair before toppling, with a thud, onto the floor.

In the house below, Diblasio's grandmother is washing a head of lettuce. She is fastidious about his diabetic's diet even though he is not. He's not allowed to keep sweets upstairs but she knows he sneaks down and eats the double-fudge homemade cookies she hides in the pantry. No matter, she says, they are for someone else. "They will kill you, Diblasio," she insists, and they did.

Above the sink is a window and out there is a long, descending backyard which slopes into a sizeable garden and ends in a marsh. The grandmother is thinking about alligators lying dormant in the mud awaiting, like her vegetables, the warm weather right around the corner. This salad she's making he'll never eat. She grips the head with both hands, digs her nails in, and begins ripping the lettuce into manageable chunks. When the house shakes from the impact of her toppling grandson above she mistakes it for her own unexpected trembling fury.

Living like a nobody is harder than it looks. It is hardest among people. It's not that people can really see Grumman—*look right through me, look right through me*—it's that he can see *them*. *They* are all around. They drive by and turn their heads to steal a peek at the young man in the black Cadillac. *Why not look?* they figure. And what do they see? A twenty-year-old weighted down by his furrowed brows and pursed lips gripping the steering wheel like he's trying to murder it, eyes dead set ahead. If people think at all, they think, *That must be his dad's car.*

"And if I don't look back," Grumman tells himself, "I won't see them. What do I care? What do I think? I think *they* don't exist. This is an empty road."

Grumman's not full-blown off the grid like the phantoms in the woods or in the desert you read about; those anarchic gorillas gurgling their own diluted piss for hydration and grinding lice between gnarly teeth for protein. Grumman's more of a suburban gypsy. He occupies spaces you leave rather than spaces you'll never go. He has become talented over time; been doing this for two years since he left for college. The trick is to always remain perfectly calm like that Buddhist kid in the jungle who sat there—maybe still sits there—ignoring the world and willing the heart to slow down to near-asystole. Just north of dead. And why not go south? Don't think he hasn't seesawed through suicide. That, though, would give the last laugh to Phineas Olsen. Death was Paddywhack's bag. So what that Grumman had a little taste? That was then; that was that. Living is daily combating what was. It's about God, Grumman guesses, or something else big. It is the belief that there are defibrillators out there humming above the world. Grumman's just waiting for someone kind enough to lower them down upon his chest.

"I mean, aren't I owed that after having my heart ripped... deserved to suffer for what he...had such hate and it can be contagious if...why that damned wooden elephant on the mantle...all so meaningless...red splatter stained forever..."

Grumman manages the car back on the road, startled by the rumble strips. This all-day-driving a stolen car out in the open has got to stop. Let's not be sloppy. Outside is twilight in Richmond. Been on fumes for miles. Every bus station in the country is situated in the seediest part of town. Grumman turns the car off and leaves the key in the ignition.

Inside the terminal, Grumman tries not to notice the people and instead looks for a destination. He'll need something on the coast, somewhere snowbirds have abandoned for the season. Kitty Hawk will do. He buys a ticket without making eye contact with anyone. He's got the money. Has enough cash to get by forever the way he's been living. It is a small condolence for the price of fanfare. Hard to blame the media. Newspapers and magazines aren't exploiting if your legal guardians—grandparents—take the money. "It's all for you," they said, and gave it to him at eighteen. Grumman buried the lion's share beneath a jungle gym in a park near his childhood home. He returns from time to time.

On the bus Grumman closes his eyes and listens to the rising shift in gears which drowns the low murmur of passengers. Sleep is easy this way. When those gears wind down, Grumman awakens. Heavy-headed, he rises and files into the aisle to wait in line with everyone else. It is still dark outside and, if he hurries, there will be enough time to find a home before sunrise.

With his eyes lowered Grumman waits for the pudgy man in front of him to move. The man is wearing a red football jersey with the number 32 stitched in black on the back. The name *Kuller* is embroidered across the man's sloped shoulders.

That name rings a bell and Grumman doesn't watch football.

And though it is something he wouldn't ordinarily dream of doing, Grumman taps the man on the shoulder and mutters, "Where did you get the shirt?"


The grandmother enters the house, closes the door, and stands breathless with her back to it. From where she is she can see into the dining room, the living room, and part of the kitchen. She dizzily casts her eyes around the space.

This is the house her husband chose so many years ago. A mostly-sequestered two-bedroom ranch with an in-law apartment above the garage. The nearest neighbor is acres away. This is where they lived and had a son. The son moved out and had a son. All these men ballooned early and grotesquely fed their fate; not suicide exactly, just an irresistible craving to devour. The grandmother is the one who fought their ravenous appetites. She committed herself to vegetables. She tended the garden. If her family would have looked at her—thin as rain—they'd have seen a portrait of self-discipline. But you are no role model when nobody sees you. You are inconsequential. Drop in bucket. So they fell: the grandmother's husband's heart burst, her son's, subsequently, did the same, and her grandson, Diblasio, the biggest of them all, moved into the in-law apartment. And now, only in his early thirties, he's out. Planted in the April earth with the others.

Without the weight of her grandson the house feels clean. She can court the secret she's kept under lock and key.

After her husband passed the grandmother started an affair with a man she met at Home Depot…her lover Leo was taking a break from his wife…seduced by her baked goods and attentiveness in the bedroom…he was her second chance and she hoped vice versa…Leslie, the wife, started to get sick…guilt and shame and all that jazz…passion for him only enflamed over the years…

Shortly after her grandson quit his job as a computer consultant and moved into the apartment with his Big Idea, Leo and Leslie became residents of the Golden Gardens retirement community. Leslie was becoming too difficult with her dementia for Leo to handle alone. The grandmother tentatively visited. Leo refused to make eye contact. He sat on the bench swing in the courtyard clinging to Leslie. If Leslie knew that the grandmother was perched on a picnic table a few feet away, it didn't show in her faraway gaze. Meanwhile, Leo quietly hummed their wedding song in Leslie's ear and tried to sway a little, desperate for his wife to remember the years of good times rather than those recent six months when he took a break from her.

Determined, the grandmother increased her visitations. She made brownies and coffeecakes and befriended some of the residents. She played bridge with Gracie and Wanda and listened to Hugh and Tim argue politics. And though Leo never budged, she learned from Victoria that he'd snatch one of her cookies after visiting hours.

As the grandmother smoothes out her blouse her hands tremble. She has never been closer to Leo than right at this moment. Her life has always been measured in the tug of time. Time to lose her husband and battle that abandonment. Time to grieve the passing of her son. Time to reinvent herself with another man. Time for Leslie to pass. Time to slide her shoulder into the comfortable curve of Leo's arm.

It's time to move into the Golden Gardens retirement community. Turns out her foul-mouthed grandson had made some money with his Big Idea, which he left to her. The nicest thing Diblasio has ever done he did when he died. It is enough to get her foot in the door. Now, as she does a two-step jig in the foyer, she just has to unload the house.


Kitty Hawk is pleasant. It is close enough to the water without being in it. There are rolling sand dunes. Tourists can learn a little something about airplanes. The Wright brothers started out by testing…ignored the naysayers who claimed…were able to reach an altitude…pioneers of aviation…

The heat soars outside. Inside, Grumman sits shirtless on the cool tile in front of a laptop computer in the dark. The owners of this house have hung hurricane shutters, just in case, and driven back to Ohio. Splinters of light creep in. Grumman has memorized just how far one beam will stretch before it retreats as the day dies. And many days have passed since Grumman climbed off the bus with someone else's computer satchel, a deep sickness in his gut, and wandered past the many foreclosing houses (places he avoids) to this home.

The first thing Grumman did once he had tapped into a wireless connection is search for himself. Right off the bat he found the unofficial Grumman Botts webpage. Someone named KitschLover manages the site. On it are many links. The first web address directs you to the *People* article. The cover photo depicts Grumman, a sixteen-year old kid, staring hollow-eyed at the camera and loosely holding a .22. That magazine article outlines the gory details of the murders. It explains what happened: Grumman, a minor insomniac, was in the kitchen pantry around midnight. He would often eat a bagful of chips to help pass through the night. His mother didn't like this habit so he hid. He didn't hear the intruder pick the front door lock, quietly step inside, first check Grumman's bedroom, the bathroom, remove the hefty knick-knack from the mantle above the fireplace, and then enter the master bedroom. He did hear the screaming. *Courage*, the journalist wrote, *is not a strong enough word for what Grumman did next.* He stepped out of the pantry, across the living room, careful not to think about what was happening to his parents or what could happen to him if he didn't hurry, and into the den where his father kept the hunting rifles. The bullets were locked in the drawer and the key was on a bookshelf. Those moments were like days as he fumbled to load the gun. He only had time for one bullet before Paddywhack, coated in slick blood, charged. He put that bullet between the killer's eyes. His dad used to take Grumman duck hunting. The article labeled him a hero. There were all kinds of letters from all kinds of people. Gun enthusiasts sent modest checks.

There are other sites. Any time Phineas Olsen is mentioned, Grumman is noted. They are inextricably linked. Phineas Olsen, also known as the Knick-Knack Killer, later dubbed "Paddywhack" by a journalist who wrote for the *Miami Herald*, started his murdering spree in Ft. Lauderdale and it ended in Indianapolis, in Grumman's family room. There are many other facts and double as many speculations surrounding the killer. Grumman has sealed all that up airtight.

The last time KitschLover updated the website was well over a year ago with a link to an article from Bloomington's *Herald Times* reporting that the college's most famous freshman had dropped out. It was nothing more than two paragraphs buried beneath local news. There haven't been any recent postings.

Satisfied, Grumman visited the site that the pudgy man on the bus told him about: www.killerjerseys.com. Killer Jerseys sells football-style shirts with the names of serial killers printed on the back and a number corresponding to confirmed victims. They come in red with black lettering or black with red lettering. Grumman thought this was a joke—what kind of person would *actually* buy them—until he read an online article about the product and a brief interview with the Killer Jerseys creator. Sales were staggering. Grumman had no idea. Teems of wannabe murderers are probably out there walking the streets right now. In the online article the entrepreneur gave his opinion about the popularity of the shirts: "People want to live dangerously. The jerseys put them in proximity. They're also great conversation-starters."

Grumman perused the online catalog. There were many choices. When you clicked on the name of a killer you could see a brief summary of the murders:

#10, Jumping Jack Pinkerton—he did several jumping jacks in the pool of his victims' blood while their life drained...

#12, Twinkle Toes—after he knifed his victims he would take off their shoes, cut their toenails, and put the shoes back on. What he did with the clippings is...

#15, Casper—an albino, he blanched his victims with buckets of bleach in an effort to cleanse...

#20, Lightning Ira Watts—she'd visit public pools late at night when lovers were fooling around in hot tubs and, with an extension cord, toss a heavy-duty electric appliance...

#24, Paddywhack...

Grumman turned the computer off. He folded his legs and prepared to enter into his trance. The way into the trance is to visualize a problem and then excise it until you're left with nothing but *your* self in *your* mind. What Grumman did was go hunting. His head is full of serial killers; from pictures he has seen online he has memorized what each devil looks like. He conjured up the .22 from his past, felt the heft of it, the smooth curve of the trigger, and then he put a bullet between Marc Rallin's eyes. He took out Randy Ship, Tod Ridgeway, Frankie Sellers, Eileen Archer—he had plenty of bullets—Jeremy Chase, Edward Landry, Sam Mosely, Dennis Delmer... *bang, bang, bang, bang, bang...*

In his feverish spree Grumman accidentally visualized the pudgy man from the bus and ventilated his skull. This wasn't inner-calm, wasting ordinary citizens. Inner calm was *blissful peace* as described by Grumman's childhood psychologist. Back then blissful peace meant nothing to Grumman. Just some shit someone says. Then, one day when he was bored and surfing the net, he discovered the Buddha Boy at www.buddhaboy. com. Here was a robed Nepalese kid around the same age as Grumman sitting prone beneath a huge peepal tree in the jungle. His hands clasped in his lap. He sat there as the day brightened and the day darkened. A tourist-turned-believer with a computer degree trained a live-feed webcast on the boy so you could look at him twenty-four-seven. Grumman visited the site religiously and waited for something to happen. Nothing ever did. Not when it rained or when bugs crawled over the boy or leopards prowled closely or the temperatures soared and then dwindled. Kid just sat in his white robe like a mannequin.

That was blissful peace.

Now, when Grumman checks on www.buddhaboy.com, the site is gone. He's not unhappy about this. Back when he stared at the boy on the screen all day Grumman felt a little guilty about it; intrusive. He was behaving a little like all the voyeurs gawking at his image in *People* magazine and prying, prying, prying. Probably, some monk reprimanded the tourist and made him disconnect the camera. Or the boy stood up, ate a sandwich, and did childish things. Maybe, now that he's older, www.buddhayoungman.com is gathering followers. Or it was all a hoax. This is not something he's going to investigate. He would like to believe that the boy just vanished, or levitated into the sky, or vaporized into a million particles of light.

What Grumman does do is hunt down Diblasio Weems, the brainchild behind Killer Jerseys. It's easy to find the address of a man with that name in the online white pages. There could be a good reason why Diblasio would do what he has done. Lots of them make sense: an ironic commentary on society's desensitization…appropriation of these monsters as a means of overcoming an irrational sense of fear…a shrewd parallel between celebrated violence on the football field with…pure capitalistic greed…

Or maybe Diblasio is the family member of a victim himself and this is a coping strategy.

Grumman tells himself to not be bothered. Who cares? Off the grid means you don't get an opinion. You have no voice. *Why not just ask him?* You spend every day protecting your ears and your eyes in order to control what you feel. What's in your head. *Make him stop.*

The ray of light touches his foot and fades. When it disappears, Grumman steps out into the night with it. Overhead a jet screeches by.

———

It isn't as simple as the grandmother thought it would be, getting herself checked into the Golden Gardens retirement home. There's a mountain of paperwork, an interview (they are sending someone to the house today or tomorrow to conduct it), a financial background check which the grandmother cannot verify until the banks have transferred all of Diblasio's money into her account which they cannot do until the lawyers and accountants settle…and the house; that's another story entirely, with the market in the toilet and places foreclosing everywhere you turn…

The grandmother carries a cool, pink washcloth out to the deck chair in the afternoon shade of the house and tries to stay calm. Glancing down the slope of her backyard she runs her fingers through her thinning, matted, gray hair. This heat wave has made her testy. The brittle centipede grass has stayed dormant in the arid weather. Her petunias look like shriveled spiders. She has no desire to haul out the rainbow sprinklers.

About the only thing the grandmother is going to miss, if she ever gets out of this place, is the vegetable garden. It has been her private retreat over the years. A place to keep her hands occupied. It is also where she first took an interest in poison. In the beginning she waged war against the weeds. She got to know the gentlemen in Lawn and Garden. They suggested this and that and she tried and tried until she got it right. Then came the nibbling rodents. There weren't very many options for exterminating varmints with poison at Home Depot. Devon, an impatient man with a receding hairline and a boat with a blown engine at home in the detached garage where wasps nested in the eaves, showed her what they had. She scattered laced tomatoes, onions, corn, and peppers on the ground like a buffet and waited. Nothing happened. The bait disappeared with no dead body in its wake. She explained this to Devon.

"What you need," Devon whispered, "is something with higher arsenic trioxide."

"Which shelf?"

"Oh, we don't carry that at the Depot."

"Do I have to describe in detail what they're doing to my cukes?"

Conspiratorially, Devon scribbled down directions to Miller's Bait n'Amo and told the grandmother to mention his name. "They'll hook you up."

The stronger stuff didn't seem to be working, either. She kept watch from the deck with a glass of pink lemonade. Sometimes, when it was late and cool, Diblasio would groan down the outside staircase to his apartment and join her.

"What are you staring at?" he asked one evening. "Got a look about you."

The grandmother told Diblasio about the mystery which didn't interest him. Instead, he said, "It must be in the blood."

"The rodents are immune?"

"No, Grandma, in your blood. Your fascination with poison. You know…"

"I wouldn't say *fascination*, I'm just protecting…"

"…you and I have a serial killer in our family. Annette Lindon, the Cough-Syrup Killer. She was cousins of your great-great grandmother. Worked as a nurse at the Fairfield hospital and really fucking hated her patients. Who knows why. Afraid of getting old herself, maybe; sometimes killers try to control their own lives by taking…"

"Are you getting bitten? I'm getting bitten. Those mosquitoes love…"

"…she'd mix Robitussin with cyanide and serve it in a little paper cup decorated with flowers. Took out a baker's dozen before they caught her. I've got a shirt upstairs. I'll get you one…"

"I'm going inside," the grandmother wailed. "I can't stand it any longer."

The next morning she found the dead alligator in her sweet potatoes with a rabbit carcass dangling from its jaws. Apparently, the poisoned rodents had been poisoning the gators. She dialed down the dosage."

"Now," she announces, "you're on your own. I'm swapping this garden for a better one." She smiles at the thought. Tonight, like she has done every evening for the past two weeks, she will visit the Golden Gardens retirement community. She's making headway. Her friends are happy to hear she'll be checking in soon. Last night she caught Leo's eye and saw his face flush.

The coolness of the washcloth evaporates. The heat is really becoming too much. Not to mention the burden of the house. The grandmother has not set foot in Diblasio's upstairs apartment since she discovered him around supper time the day he died. She wasn't surprised, of course, and had time to tidy up his disheveled apartment before the ambulance arrived and difficultly carted him off. The grandmother felt such shame when she saw the strain it caused several paramedics to get him down the rickety outside staircase. She whispered many apologies.

Rising, feeling the burden of her age, the grandmother gets lightheaded. She puts a speckled arm against the vinyl siding to keep from falling and, exposed like that, an idea blossoms.

"Let's just think this through," she says to herself as she struggles into the house. "Got to make sure the insurance is updated and that I'll get enough to supplement what Diblasio has left. It has got to look like an accident; you can't just douse the place with gasoline…"

Then she is startled to see the outline of a stranger in the

foyer. She blinks rapidly and covers her mouth with the washcloth waiting to see what is what here.

"Your door wasn't all-the-way closed when I knocked," the
young man says.

"Oh." The grandmother tries to gain her composure. "I was
on the deck and couldn't hear. You must be from Golden Gardens."

As her eyes adjust, the grandmother scrutinizes her company. He is tall and thin like a mantis. He is clasping his hands
in front of himself as if he is holding a formal hat. But he isn't
carrying anything. His hair leaps down to his shoulders in curls
and now that she has had a chance to look closely she can tell
by the old clothes he's wearing that he is not from the retirement community.

"Is Diblasio home?"

"Won't you have a seat now that you're inside?"

The young man doesn't budge. He remains unblinkingly
still, staring off at something on the horizon outside.

"All right, then. I am going to sit if it's all the same to you."
The grandmother shimmies onto a stool at the counter in the
kitchen where the cordless is within reach. "And, no," she answers, lifting her chin. "He's not here."

"When will he return?"

"Oh, he's definitely not the Second Coming," she says, then
snorts. "So, never."

The grandmother studies the expression on the man's face
as he tries to make sense of her comment. When he does, his
shoulders slump, his head falls, and his arms droop loosely.
The grandmother waits. The front door is partially open and
the sticky heat is advancing around the young man into the air
conditioning. She can see he's trying hard to decide what to do.
If she had a boy with a man like her it'd look like this stranger.

He is simple to read: a loner who indirectly knew her grandson, probably from the internet…too beautiful in his sadness to know Diblasio well…estranged from his mother, clearly, the way he…in need of a shoulder and a shower…nowhere else to be; nowhere else to go…came here out of desperation…

"All right," the young man says, turning his back to her and stepping out the front door.

The grandmother pinches her lips together in consternation. She's not sure what that was all about. Diblasio didn't have many visitors. *No matter*, she thinks, *there are more pressing issues*. She puts her arm on the kitchen counter and her head in her hand. This gives her a clear view into her dark bedroom where the automatic night light is illuminated. She stares and stares. Eventually, she sees a cockroach scuttle up from the baseboard in her bedroom and fret upon the wall. Ordinarily, the grandmother would fetch a can of Raid from the cabinet and spritz the thing. Not this evening, though. Instead, she studies it. Surely, there are more lingering beneath the surface. Her walls are crawling.

Grumman doesn't know what the hell he is doing in Diblasio Weems' apartment, his back to the door, breathing evening, with the old woman below. If you squat in a place while it's occupied, you're an intruder. You're just one delicate step away from something sinister.

Earlier this afternoon, after Grumman left the house, he began his trek back to the bus station, walking along the shoulder of the county road, past the Fish Shack, crunching through the dry, brittle, Carolina whistle-grass. That the son-of-a-bitch who made the shirts was dead threw Grumman for a loop. He tried to explain to himself that this is why he came in the first place—in a round-about way—to convince Diblasio to stop making Paddywhack jerseys. Now that's done. Of course, someone else will make them. They are too profitable to ignore, Grumman knows this and it doesn't matter—*Oh well, whatever, never mind*—he's not going to chase after the next capitalistic parasite. *Fuck it.*

Grumman can't quite pinpoint the reason he stopped mid-stride—a Buick passing with passengers he did not see leering at the unlucky fool outside in all this heat—but lots of them make sense: to sit down and maybe comfort a grieving old woman who has lost…help her move boxes and sort through his things…find out what kind of man Diblasio had been other than a Hawker of Jerseys, an Exploiter of Victims, a Serial Killer groupie…if only he could have gotten his hands on him before he died…didn't know how he passed in the first place…

*Hard to say*, Grumman thinks, using the bolts Diblasio had installed inside his apartment to shut himself in. He's here now having waited in the woods until nightfall, silently creeping up the outside staircase, and picking the simple lock. He stands for a while and soaks the place in. The air is musty and sour. A stab of moonlight pokes through a bend in the blinds. There are a mountain of boxes against the back wall—Killer Jerseys waiting to be delivered. There's a pathway cutting between the boxes which leads to a bathroom. Just in front of him is a swivel chair which Grumman uses to rest a moment. It occurs to him that he is exhausted. At the computer desk is a monitor and a potted cactus. Underneath the desk are a mini-fridge and the CPU. He opens the fridge and finds a canister of sodium-free peanuts which he munches as he waits for the computer to come alive.

Grumman can't discern much about Diblasio's personal life

from the desktop. There are no pictures or meaningful quotations. What he does find are serial killer files in beige folders set against a wavy-gray background. Inside are details about the murders and speculations about the motivations. There are crime scene photographs. Grumman scrolls through. He has done his own investigating through the years in order to help visualize the monsters. Most of this is old hat—*Tell me something I don't know.*

In a folder labeled *Death Row* Grumman browses the names of the many murderers who have been executed. Curious, he double clicks the *Last Meals* folder and skims some of the orders killers placed before dying…Bobbie Lions—pizza, meatballs, and a Pepsi…Ian McMurray—four pieces of fried chicken (white meat), five pieces of deep fried fish, four deep fried breaded pork chops, extra-large order of french fries, ketchup, tarter sauce, one pint Blue Bell Peanut Butter Crunch ice cream, two quarts of chocolate milk…Perry Duncan—rib eye steak, a baked potato with sour cream and butter, hush puppies, a Coke and pecan pie…Gary White—requested no last meal, eating only an ice cream sandwich from a vending machine…Tony Hawes—two chili cheese dogs, two cheeseburgers, two orders of onion rings with Ranch dressing, a turkey salad, egg rolls, chocolate cake, apple pie, one peach, three Dr. Pepper sodas, jalapenos…

The night Paddywhack murdered his parents, Grumman's mother baked meatloaf with a ketchup glaze, scalloped potatoes, French-style green beans, buttermilk biscuits, and they each drank one glass of boxed red wine. Grumman's sure this information doesn't mean a thing. He screws the cap back on the peanuts and places them in the fridge. He turns the computer off and curls beneath the desk. The buzz of the machine powering down sends him under.

The sound of a car door slamming wakes Grumman up. He wearily rises and walks to the window in the bathroom to peer out. It's bright with plumes of heat bounding off the hood of the old lady's green Crown Victoria. Slash pine trees tickle the horizon in a sway. Clouds in the sky look like something a dog chewed up and then spit out angry. She single-mindedly backs out of the drive and doesn't bother to glance up and see Grumman gawking plain-as-day. He uses the bathroom, sets his clothes aside and takes a shower. Diblasio has dandruff shampoo and a bar of Zest soap. Afterwards, Grumman rummages through the boxes of jerseys until he finds number 24. It is sizes too big and oddly comfortable this way.

Returning to the center of the room, Grumman lowers himself to the floor to stretch. In the daylight he can see the deep depressions in the carpet from the wheels on the swivel chair. Once he is loose, Grumman sits upright, places one foot on top of his thigh and the other foot in front of his lower leg. Then he presses down on his knees, works his legs to the floor, and pulls his lower leg on top of his inner thigh. Arms drape down to the knees. Breathing slows. Eyes close. Grumman weaves in. It has never been easier to find that self place, guided by the dead.

Later in the evening when the grandmother returns from Home Depot with a dozen insect fumigators, Grumman doesn't hear. She dons her best jewelry and easily packs a bag full of photo albums, toiletries, and clothes. There is so very little she will miss. Then she carefully shatters the glass bulb on the night light with a teaspoon so that the filament is exposed. With the shades parted she will have three hours before it is dark enough for the damaged light to pop on. Then, if you are to believe the warnings on the back of the foggers and defy them, boom. For good measure, she triggers all of the bug bombs in her bedroom, seals the door, and leaves. When tired authorities and insurance investigators half-heartedly sift through the ashes and find nothing more than the coagulated remains of the mini-fridge and ask, "Why so many?" she'll reply, voice wavering, responsible for 30,000 acres of loss, "I wanted to make sure I got them all."

Before that, though, upstairs, Grumman takes the insecticide into his lungs. He is too busy cycling through and imagining the different ways that food can choke a man to taste the poison. Cockroaches clamor toward the ceiling in a panic he doesn't feel. He succeeds in feeling nothing at all until his chest glows with warmth.

# INSECTUALITY

Arc went into the city to soothe a woman's hands. Her name was Muir. She entered the bakery wearing a scarf and sunglasses one afternoon and pointed to a pastry filled with cream, behind the glass. Arc began to fetch the pastry and just when he had the cellophane paper firmly gripped on the item Muir said, "Not that one, that one." And she pointed again, this time to a croissant clearly on a different tray from the cream-filled pastry. Her hand had a long pointer finger which she smudged on the glass casing emphasizing the croissant. But when Arc retrieved it, Muir said, "No, no, that's not what I meant at all." Finally, she bought a glazed doughnut and a cup of cranberry-flavored hot tea which she consumed with a look of disdain standing in the shop and gazing out the window at the autumn decorations lining the street.

This became routine. Muir wanted a glazed doughnut every other day and Arc was there to provide it. If Arc went for the doughnut first, Muir would bite her lip, considering, and say, "No, I don't think so," and she'd point to an everything bagel that she didn't want and in time return to the glazed doughnut. Sometimes she drank flavored coffee, differently flavored by her whim.

Arc didn't mind the trouble. He found her faux-indecision alluring. It seemed like she didn't know what she wanted when really she just needed the time to listen to her desires. He wanted to believe love worked like this. He compared himself to the glazed doughnut and thought, at closing as he mopped, *I am like the glazed doughnut. Muir probably dates a lot. I'm not her type, certainly. I'm not handsome. I don't have a good head of hair. But that's the stuff on the outside. Inside, I'm as good as anyone. She chooses the doughnut in the end. I can fix my glaze.*

Wearing a paper hat was a requirement at the bakery. Arc knew this, he understood the dress requirements. Once, though, Muir pointed to Arc's head and said, "Your hat is crooked." Then she pointed to a roll she couldn't decide on. Arc checked his reflection in the window and colored when he saw how clownish the lopsided hat made him look. He straightened it and reached for the roll she didn't want.

Two days later Arc wore a black pork pie hat tilted just so. Muir said, offhandedly, "Something about you is different." Arc beamed and whistled softly as he went from an éclair to a loaf of sourdough bread and then to the glazed doughnut.

The boss, Mr. Darbray, reprimanded Arc and it was back to the paper hat. Still, Arc kept his pork pie hidden in an unused drawer under the counter and donned it when he saw Muir in her slow pace down the street toward the bakery.

The first time Arc asked Muir for a date, he was nervous. He said, "Would you like to go out on a date?"

She said, "No, I think I'll have the glazed doughnut. And a cup of hot cider."

Arc figured Muir heard, *Would you like a piece of cake?* He'd have to be more articulate.

The second time Arc asked Muir for a date she simply said, "No."

This didn't bother Arc, he knew it wouldn't be easy. He did sit-ups at home and brushed his teeth after meals. He bought a glossy magazine which claimed to know one hundred and one ways to a woman's heart. Arc only needed one so he chose, *Be confident!* In his apartment he practiced reaching into the refrigerator, keeping his arm straight, and saying, "Would you like to try a Danish?" in a deep voice. "Perhaps the hot fresh French bread just out of the oven?"

The next time he asked her out she said, "No."

Arc bought cologne. He shaved twice a day and when she rejected him again, he didn't shave though this got him in trouble with Darbray. He tried acting coy, disinterested. When she pointed her finger at a muffin he pretended it was no big deal. At the end of the night, mopping, he thought, *Damn, damn, damn.*

Two days later Mr. Darbray said he was going into the city for a dough convention and asked Arc to lock up that evening. Arc waited until he saw Muir coming down the street in her scarf and sunglasses. He grabbed his pork pie hat and hurried outside to lock the door.

Muir stopped next to Arc and said, "What's this?"

"Oh," Arc said casually, "we had to close early. Something came up."

She tried the door anyway. It was locked.

"There is a place around the corner that makes wonderful doughnuts," Arc said.

Muir folded her arms.

"I feel badly. Let me buy you a doughnut. It's just a block away."

Her scarf blew gently over her shoulder.

Arc began walking backward, beckoning Muir. "Come on," he said, "it's a magnificent day."

Muir reluctantly followed at a slow pace. She had on blue shoes.

The place sold doughnuts only. Arc figured it would take her a while to get to the glazed kind. He wanted to put on his pork pie hat and the cologne he kept in his baker's apron, so Arc excused himself and made for the bathroom. When he tried the door a man said, "I'm in here," harshly. Arc waited. He put the hat on and tried to tilt it properly. He checked his image in his watch. Things were out of proportion. And the seconds were ticking. Eventually, Arc heard flushing in the bathroom and was surprised when the door opened before the sound of running water or the automatic dryer; obviously he didn't wash up in there. A large man stepped from the bathroom and scowled.

"She's all yours," the man said, patting Arc roughly on the back.

Inside, the bathroom had a tremendous stink. And the mirror had an odd film over it. Arc fiddled with his hat and tried to hold his breath. Then he put on cologne. Then he worried if he was going to smell like both the cologne and the large man's bowel movement. Arc washed up. Another man entered the bathroom. He looked Arc over and said, "Hoo, boy!"

Muir had eaten half her glazed doughnut and was seated at a table against the wall. Arc joined her.

"Hi," he said. "Sorry. I wanted to pay for that."

"Don't be silly," Muir said.

Arc took out his wallet. "Please, let me pay. What was it three dollars?"

"You're not paying for it. I make an honest living."

Arc put his wallet away. "What do you do, anyway?"

Muir pushed her sunglasses down enough to gaze over them at Arc. "I'm an actress."

"Really? You look like a movie star."

"Well, I'm not in the pictures yet. I'm in plays."

"Plays are good, too. I mean, you've got to be spontaneous, I'll bet. All those lines to memorize."

"I don't have any lines."

Muir finished eating. The large man from the bathroom sat down with a tray full of jelly doughnuts at a table just behind Muir, facing Arc. He watched Arc with heavy-lidded eyes and began cramming food in his mouth.

"Oh. No lines. Well, I'm sure you'll get some."

"Nobody has lines. It's performative. And experimental. It's called *The Dreamlife of Insects*."

The large man licked his fingers and stared.

"It's about dreaming bugs?"

"Insects," Muir emphasized.

"Which kind are you?"

Muir pushed her sunglasses up. She stood, tossed her scarf around her shoulders, and prepared to leave. "Depends on the night."

That night Arc read about bugs. Then he bought an ant farm. He watched the ants make their little homes and dreamt of possibilities. When Muir next came in he casually remarked, "Oh how I love the sound of katydids on a crisp October night!"

Muir didn't comment. She pointed to raisin bread.

Arc sighed. He went for the bread.

She said, "On second thought…" and pointed to a cannoli.

Arc said, "Would you like to go out on a date?"

Muir said, "No. And you know what, I think I'll take the glazed doughnut."

"Of course you will," Arc said, frustrated. "Could you tell me why?"

Muir pushed her sunglasses down and sized Arc up. Arc stood on his toes and tried to relax his shoulders.

"You look like my brother," she said.

"Oh." Arc placed the glazed doughnut on the counter.

"I'll take hot chocolate today."

"Is your brother nice?" Arc asked.

"He's fine."

"Do women find him attractive?"

"One woman did, I guess. He's married."

Muir turned her back and carried her hot chocolate and glazed doughnut over to the window. An old woman entered the store and ordered coffeecake. Arc rang her up. She started to pay in low change. Arc couldn't wait to get her out of the bakery. Muir slurped her hot chocolate. She bit the glazed doughnut.

"Just take it," Arc whispered to the woman.

"What?"

"It's on the house," Arc insisted, as he set the cake in her hands.

The lady said, "It's all right, I've got some pennies at the bottom of my purse." She dug in.

Muir was gazing thoughtfully into her cup.

"More hot chocolate?" Arc asked.

"I didn't order hot chocolate," the woman said. "I just want the coffeecake."

"I know ma'am, I was talking to the young lady behind you."

Muir didn't move. The old woman finally paid and walked out of the bakery mumbling to herself.

Alone again with Muir, Arc asked, "Is your brother happy?"

"He's in Pennsylvania," she replied.

Arc didn't know how to take this so he nodded and nodded.

As he mopped Arc tried to remember the capital of Pennsylvania. Later he borrowed an encyclopedia from his old neighbor who liked facts. He learned that Harrisburg was the capital. He discovered that Pennsylvania was one of the original thirteen colonies. He memorized the state bird, motto, tree, and population.

When Muir came into the bakery next, Arc said, "Did you know Louisa May Alcott was from Pennsylvania?"

Muir said, "Who?" She indicated cheesecake behind the glass.

"She wrote *Little Women*."

"Never read it."

"Me neither. Sounds good, though."

"You know, I don't think I'll take the cheesecake. Give me pumpkin pie."

"What do you think of, 'Virtue, Liberty and Independence?'"

"What?"

"It's Pennsylvania's motto."

"When I was there those things weren't," Muir said dramatically.

"What do you mean?"

"It's not easy being a woman in rural Pennsylvania."

Arc accidentally stuck his thumb in the pumpkin pie. "Interesting," he said. "May I ask why?"

"You couldn't possibly understand."

"Because I'm a man?"

"I'll stick with the glazed doughnut," Muir said, pointing.

"Help me understand."

"The doughnut with the glaze. Right there."

"You, I meant. I mean, understand you. Help me."

Muir ignored this, paid, ate her doughnut and left.

That night, for punishment, Arc wrote the sentence, *Help me understand you* one thousand times in a notebook. The pain he felt in his hand the next day was a small victory.

Muir didn't come into the bakery for a week. When she did, Arc hadn't had time to get under his pork pie hat. He had been powdering doughnuts and was a mess. Flustered, Arc blurted, "It's great to see you again."

Muir smiled weakly. She looked irritated. Arc noticed her gloves. When she pointed her finger to the glass casing at a peanut butter cookie, she scratched her hand. Arc snatched the cookie like a pro. Muir stomped her foot, said, "No, no." She pointed to cornbread, removed her gloves and scratched her hands unmercifully. Through the glass casing, over the cornbread, Arc regarded the red rash and blisters on her skin. Her nails dug deeply. Arc swallowed hard. Muir quickly put her gloves back on.

"It's just the chicken pox," Muir said. "It'll go away soon."

Arc straightened himself, scratched his own hands instinctively. "No, I think the pox is a child's condition."

"It's the chicken pox," Muir insisted, as she swiveled toward the door.

"Hey, no," Arc said. "It's just a rash. Don't leave."

Muir rushed outside and up the street.

Arc checked up on chicken pox. He was right, it normally affected kids. *Stranger things have happened*, Arc decided. He bought a bottle of calamine lotion for Muir's hands. He kept it in his pouch. Muir didn't come. Mopping, Arc thought, *Maybe the day after tomorrow.*

The day after tomorrow passed. Arc worried about the rash as a week went by. Customers pointed to things behind the casing and Arc purposefully grabbed the wrong items in memory of Muir. This frustrated them. One customer, who was sleeping with Mr. Darbray, squealed on Arc. Darbray threatened termination if attitudes weren't adjusted. Arc found it impossible to adjust without Muir. All the pastries reminded him of her. Another week passed and nothing good happened. He bought a city paper and found information on *The Dreamlife of Insects*. In a spurred moment he wrote, *So long, Doughboy*, on a paper napkin and left the bakery early.

On his way to the florist Arc saw several houses in a row that had black plastic eagles over their garages. He tried to buy a mountain laurel from the florist. He explained that it was Pennsylvania's state flower. The best the florist could do was a rhododendron. Arc bought it.

On his way to the bus stop Arc noticed wind chimes on nearly every porch. They made noise. Leaves on the sidewalk scratched the concrete. The sky turned an honest purple promising a storm.

On the bus Arc put his pork pie hat on just so, using the window as a mirror. Outside buildings leapt to the darkening sky. Arc read the back of the calamine lotion bottle. It was supposed to calm the itch. He wondered why the stuff was pink.

Off the bus, the wind played through the city and threatened to tear Arc's hat from his head. Rain introduced night. *The Dreamlife of Insects* was not playing on the main drag. It was in an old movie theater, which Arc passed twice without noticing. This made him late. The ticket-taker breathed so loudly Arc had to raise his voice to purchase the expensive pass. The performance was through double doors.

The theater had three sections and a balcony. There was a decent crowd, Arc noticed, and a scent of perfume. It was darker than he thought necessary. A spotlight darted erratically across the stage. Arc walked a few feet down the aisle and realized that everybody on stage was naked. Except Muir. She had on red arm-length gloves. Including Muir, four women crawled across the stage. Near the front, a musician played a viola. The sound was meant to be creepy. Arc's arms dropped to his side. The rhododendron nearly touched the floor.

Actresses rubbed themselves and rolled over each other. The spotlight pinned Muir. She was on her back, stretching her legs out, arms up. The three other women positioned themselves in a circle next to her. They put their legs up and their arms flat to the stage. They turned into a spider. Muir's red arms were supposed to be fangs and her body was the open mouth. Eight legs thrashed. From above, a huge white net descended until it rest on their feet. Somehow a rope got between Muir's legs. The person on the viola sawed the strings frantically, creating a buzzing noise. A woman behind Muir, hands nearly out of sight, pulled the rope. Stage left a small naked man with a pair of rubber fly wings stumbled into view. He had a huge eye-mask over his head. The rope was tied around his waist. He went this way and that way, faux-struggling. Muir shook her arms. Arc imagined they itched terribly. Obviously the rash had spread. *Calamine lotion should be applied soon before things got out of hand*, Arc reasoned. The naked fly-man moved closer to Muir. A bigger fly-man came out attached to the rope, stage left. Then another, and still more, each increasing in size. Arc wondered if they'd ever stop. Spiders didn't just gorge themselves to death. The women's legs kicked faster as the first fly-man got on his hands and knees and crawled between Muir's arms and over her body. Arc saw their genitalia touch for a moment. Then the spider swallowed him. The viola sawed faster.

Arc thought, *Maybe this isn't a good idea.*

A booming voice from a megaphone backstage chanted, "Come into my parlor said the spider to the fly. Come, come, come." The viola went berserk.

This was the first time Arc had seen Muir without sunglasses. She had a look of worn triumph on her face.

Arc stepped down the aisle. He slipped into a row and found a seat. The seat was warm as if it had been waiting for him. Or warm as if someone had just gotten up and walked away.

He sat and tried to enjoy the show. He couldn't understand why the women had to be a naked spider. He felt uncomfortable watching the larger and larger bare fly-men in their tiny wings. He looked at his knees and thought, *I'm not very cultured.*

Eventually the man on the megaphone stopped chanting, the fly-men disappeared, the net was lifted above the stage with the women holding on, and the viola ceased. A curtain dropped. The spotlight widened to cast a soft light over the entire stage and the audience applauded. Arc set the calamine and rhododendron on the sticky floor and clapped his hands. The women came out in robes to curtsy. Muir curtsied twice. Then the fly-men came out in shorts and one by one, bowed.

The lights came up and Arc noticed he was underdressed. Most men had ties and jackets and no hats. Women wore nice skirts. Arc tried to get backstage. He was shown the exit. Outside rain fell and splattered off the streets. Arc made his way to the back of the theater. He saw a door he assumed the actors used to exit. He waited in shadows against a wall. The rhododendron was damaged in the heavy rain. His pork pie hat did what it could to keep the wet off Arc's face. The door opened and laughter spilled out. Huddled actors hurried toward the street. Muir was not among them. She came out beneath the arm of one of the muscular fly-men who carried a striped umbrella.

"Muir," Arc said, stepping forward.

The fly-man was startled and stepped in front of Muir.

"I'm a friend," Arc stated.

The fly-man didn't relax.

"I work at the bakery."

"Do you know this creep?" the fly-man asked.

Muir pushed her sunglasses down and tried to place Arc. "I recognize that hat," she said. "He works at the bakery."

"I brought you a rhododendron. It's the closest they had to the mountain laurel."

The fly-man rolled his eyes. He took Muir's gloved hand.

"That flower looks beaten," Muir said.

"It's been through a lot."

"I don't want it."

Arc tossed the rhododendron aside. "You probably get flowers all the time."

"Why did you come here?"

"You haven't been to the bakery in a while. I thought you might need calamine for your rash."

"You have a rash?" the fly-man asked.

"It's the chicken pox and I already have some. It doesn't work."

"I could find something stronger."

"No, don't. It just needs time. Go home."

"I agree. Everything takes time. You need extra time to decide at the bakery, but you always figure it out. One day you'll see I'm like the glazed doughnut."

"Is it contagious?" the fly-man asked.

"It's on my arms, that's why I've been wearing gloves. You can be so dense sometimes." Muir took her hand back and folded her arms. She turned to Arc and said, "Good-bye."

"See you at the bakery," Arc said lifting his hat.

Muir turned and walked away. The fly-man had to hurry to keep her under the umbrella. For a moment their feet made impressions in the wet street before the rain washed them away.

The next morning Arc begged for his job back. Darbray said the comment about his weight hurt. Arc tried to explain himself but didn't really know how. He clasped his hands and lowered his head like in prayer. Darbray wasn't religious, but he forgave Arc. With conditions. Everything needed to be cleaned. And Darbray installed a pivoting security camera to keep an eye on Arc.

Arc didn't mind. He considered his journey into the city a success. He had written down a list of complementary things to say about Muir's part in *The Dreamlife of Insects*. First, he would mention how lovely her eyes were.

With a ladder, Arc could reach the air vents. He had a wire brush and a small bucket of soapy water which he used to clean between the slats. He worked his way from the middle into the corners. He thought about a future with Muir. Someday he'd own the bakery, she'd be his wife, and the children would be plump and happy with homemade pastries.

Arc bumped his head on the security camera. He nearly dropped the bucket and fell, but managed to hold on and regain his balance. He looked into the insect-black lens of the camera to adjust his paper hat. His image multiplied and refracted in the security camera's faceted eye. In that instant the bakery was filled with miniature Arcs all holding a bucket with a crooked hat and glazed-over eyes. Then the camera swung away and Arc was left alone.

# MAX

Crows arrive heavy as always. The mid-November sky over Auburn turns from gray-blue to black-sheen as the birds by the tens of thousand settle in. Most people here hate to hear the shrill caws and the thump of wings punishing the air. It's the sound of something ending. The birds will stay until everything freezes over and they're forced to shrug off south. While the crows blanket Auburn citizens keep their faces contorted into scowls and their shoulders and necks hunched as if they're ready to crouch and spring and extend into the sky.

Puckering his lips in consternation, Torrance Graff scoots off the school bus and hurries home under the weight of his backpack. He is a fast boy, the second fastest in the fourth grade, and can keep up with most kids on bikes when he wants to. Houses on the sheepish county road are few and far between. The plots of land are too big to bother sculpting along the property lines where eager trees have scuttled up in clumps and pitch leaves into the above ground pools sagging behind the raised-ranches. These trees here are not big enough to interest more than a few dozen crows at a time. One bird winks by Torrance, lands, and hops in a neighbor's driveway pecking gravel. The boy adjusts his backpack and unzips his coat. It is not yet cold enough for the kind of thing his mother made him wear this morning. A jacket would have been fine.

The mother is waiting for Torrance at the end of the drive with five other mothers. The women are armed with rifles and shotguns and slingshots. Torrance's mother holds a hunting bow and a quiver of arrows thin as knitting needles. They are wearing new black hunting jackets with the word MAC's embroidered in red thread on the back. Torrance's mother did the stitching in July. These are the Mothers Against Crows. Somebody had to do something after what happened to Torrance's older brother. There are still a few more mothers—Linda and Katharyn and Barb—finishing chores that the MAC's will fetch soon.

"How was school?" Torrance's mother asks as her boy humps up. The mother used to be beautiful. Now she is super-thin with matted hair and fierce eyes. There are wrinkles in her cheeks from her weird wide smile.

Torrance can't concentrate. He needs to use the bathroom.

"What did you learn today?" says another mother, a bruiser.

"I need to pee," Torrance whispers to his shoes.

"They're doing state capitals," a woman answers. Her daughter Ruby is in Torrance's class.

"What's the capital of Nebraska?" Torrance's mother asks suddenly in a pitch that quiets the women. The mothers hold their weapons awkwardly waiting. They pray Torrance knows the answer. A complicated wind sneaks around a stand of fir and rattles the clip holding the semi-erect American flag at half-mast. The flag hasn't been raised full since early January when Max passed.

Torrance doesn't say anything.

"They're going alphabetically," the other mother says in order to not make this a big deal. "Only up to Indiana, from what I understand."

"That's an easy one," the bruiser says.

"Yes it is," Torrance's mother pinches through her smile. Her eyes unwaver from her boy.

"Can I go?" Torrance asks.

"*May* I," a mother corrects.

"Dad's got church this afternoon and will be home around six to make dinner. I'll be back by seven."

"With a bagful of crow!" a mother on the periphery hollers. The women hoot and shake their pieces.

"Stay inside."

"May I play in the yard?"

"Nebraska?"

"It's Lincoln, Mom."


The Graff house has been fortified against crows. There's razor-wire stapled on the roof tiles and fake plastic owls perched on the porch. The yard has a half-dozen scarecrows with faces the mother carefully crafted to look frightening. Torrance helped water down the ground to make it soft so the father could drive the scarecrow-sticks in. So far this season the crows have stayed away from the home. Torrance knows if they do come, the mother will turn them into pincushions. She has spent several hours in the backyard every morning improving her aim and can riddle a cigarette pack from sixty yards, no problem.

Torrance takes his shoes off before entering the house. Inside, it smells floral from the jars and jars of potpourri the mother puts out. He sets his backpack in the foyer and parts the living room drapes to watch the MAC's situate their weapons in the back of their minivan before filing in and pulling away. Auburn's annual crow hunt runs for five days and this is day one. Last year the mother didn't participate. Much has changed since then.

Torrance uses the bathroom, swats down a cowlick, and heads outside. He walks along the county road past the cemetery and toward the pumpkin field. In the field are hundreds of pumpkins scattered like tumors. What the farmer wanted to sell for Halloween he's already taken and won't bother with the rest. When he passes, from the school bus window, Torrance has been watching one particular pumpkin, on the other side of the field, grow. While the other pumpkins are in various stages of letting go, this one seems to be expanding. For two weeks Torrance has wanted to investigate, which was impossible under his mother's scrutiny. Torrance has strict boundaries that do not include here.

Now, though, with the crow hunt, there is a window.

With a rush of excitement, the boy dashes out into the field. He leaps over pumpkins and dances around grappling vines. The ground is dry with the exception of occasional pockets of water where the earth dips dramatically. Clods of dirt shake loose in Torrance's footfalls.

A few non-crows peck at one or two of the seeping gourds and snatch the seeds. Crows won't trouble themselves with the thick rind. Until the pumpkins are ready to concede defeat and spill their guts, they'll stay away. Two big jays tussle in the drainage ditch. Torrance reaches the pumpkin sooner than he thought he would. Up close, it is not as big as he thinks it should be. From the road, he was imagining tractor-tire size, something he could hollow-out and hide within. What he's standing next to is the size of a medicine ball. It barely reaches his waist. Slumping against it, Torrance puts his hand to his chin and puckers his lips. On the other side of the field, beyond the drainage ditch, is a high fence which circumscribes the dump. The city has planted trees around the fence line in an effort to block the view, but the trees are still young and Torrance can see the soft mound of trash rising up to the sky. Between the implacable clouds and the waste buzzards and gulls circle and dive and fight. Sometimes a flock of pugnacious crows will fly over to push the bigger birds down the hill.

Most of the time the wind blows westward at the setting sun and keeps the stink of the place off the houses.

Torrance turns back to survey the field for the possibility of something larger than what he's got here. He's old enough not to get his hope up. It really is too late for anything to grow. Now is the wilting season, which is a shame. Soon all the pumpkins will droop back into the ground. For Halloween, the mother had dominated the single pumpkin they carved, leery of a blade in her son's hands. Torrance is not a baby and resents being treated as such. He is a trooper. He can handle a knife. He can take care of himself after school. He is not frail like his older brother had been. He's fine—maybe too often anxious—but mostly all right.

A brown sedan drives down the county road in a huff of dirt. It is his father's car. Torrance drops to his knees and hides behind the pumpkin. He should not be home so soon—it is not nearly six. Still, make no mistake, it is him. The old man bobs his head in time with something on the radio. He's drumming his long fingers against the wheel pretending he's in the band. He's wearing his dusty-brown hat which he believes he looks good in. He's of the mind that people trust a man in a good hat and since he is a real estate agent, trust is his business. He needs to be believable—*This is the best darn house in the county, a real steal*—and knows deep down everyone wants to believe. Here in the dead season, though, there haven't been houses to sell. The work grinds to a halt.

When the father has passed, Torrance bolts. He cuts through the field and flies over the small graveyard—staying clear of Max's headstone. It is a miracle he doesn't trip. By the time the father is in the drive, Torrance is midway through and in full stride. All the boy needs to do is skip over a few more graves, scale a shoddy retaining wall, and wiggle through the bushes.

Then he's in his yard.

And the father is there waiting for him, a smirk stitched across his face, among the scarecrows, arms folded.

"Go on and catch your breath," the father says.

Torrance puts his hands on his hips and gulps at the air.

"You're fast when you want to be." The father slides his hands into his jacket pocket. "Get you onto the track team."

"I'm fine," Torrance says.

"I saw you."

"Don't tell Mom."

"I came home to change, not to check up on you. I didn't expect this."

"I'm fine, Dad."

"You're surprised."

"Winded."

"I normally keep a change of clothes in the trunk, right?"

"How would I know?"

The father works at his tie.

Torrance feels a wave of heat pass beneath his collar. Running in this coat is all wrong.

"I need a change of clothes," the father states.

"Congratulations," Torrance offers.

"Don't."

"What do you want?"

"Get in the car."

"Mom will freak."

"I won't tell if you won't tell."

"It's going to be like that?"

The father offers his palms. "Get in the car."

The streets of downtown Auburn are lined with churches—Baptist, Methodist, Lutheran, Presbyterian, Pentecostal, Greek Orthodox. The tallest and most ornate among them is the Catholic Church with its spires and stained glass and golden trim. Outside the church, a congregation of volunteers has gathered and Torrance and the father join them.

The priest is glad they could make it. "This is good, honest work," he says. He pats a shrinking woman on the shoulder and backs into the church.

"OK," the woman says. "There are goggles and face masks and gloves. Wear these items at all times. Cory has already filled the wash buckets—thank you, Cory—so let's get started."

Torrance halfheartedly slides into the gear. The father grabs a ladder and holds it for Cory's father to climb high. Two other ladders are erected. Torrance sullenly grabs a brush and begins scrubbing a portion of the wall the woman points toward.

The walls of the church are splattered with crow shit—like cream of wheat—all up and down the building. At night, the birds clamor to the top of the church to sleep. In the morning they desecrate. Churchgoers and clergy members don't know how to thwart them. They've blasted hymnal music from a boombox atop the roof from dusk to dawn. They scattered shards of glass. They applied heavy prayer. None of this works. Crows aren't nitwits. The church is willing to do anything short of killing the critters. Even still, last year an unfamiliar man who carried a briefcase talked privately with Father Lance after hours. Rumor has it there were vials of poison in the case. That's all talk. The righteous thing to do is turn the other cheek and scrub every afternoon.

When it gets down to it, people in Auburn understand that the crows won't change. They've been doing the same thing as long as anyone can remember. After the birds spend the day around the lake eating or by the dump fighting, they all gather in Morrowbie's field to socialize. The Morrowbies can't do anything about it. People say the Morrowbies don't really mind and people are not wrong. It's free fertilizer. In the early evenings Mr. and Mrs. Morrowbie sit out on the back porch drinking and watching the hypnotic wave of loud birds bend. Hunters have pleaded with the family to have access to the field which Mr. Morrowbie will not yield. So, the hunters congregate on the property line between the Morrowbie field and the Jukes field where a good number of crows weigh down the boughs in an oak cluster. Mr. Jukes is an avid huntsman and an active member of the Auburn Hunting Association. He boasts that he'll eat anything he kills and says munching crow once and a while is something everyone should do. The hunters will pick at the pocket of birds in the oak and bide time. Then, when the birds decide it's time—based on some bird logic—platoons by the hundreds lift from the Morrowbie field and fly over the Jukes field on their way downtown. And that's when the hunters really have at it.

Torrance makes sweeping concentric circles over an area of bleached stone. If his mother only knew. The droppings are infested with bacteria. The mother's sure the crows are to blame for shoving Max over the edge. Someone, she's sure, stepped in the mess and tracked it into the house where her oldest son was paying the price of chemotherapy. With a weakened immunity, psittacosis in the crow crap infiltrated Max's system to give him pneumonia. He'd combat the infection for nearly seven weeks. This is how the mother sees it. She has since been anxious for the birds return.

The father is not sure why his wife hasn't turned her wrath upon him. If anyone tracked crow shit into the house, he did. He's the one most exposed. He's been scrubbing the church walls for years. All it would have taken was a speck or smaller. How big is a germ? If it would make his wife feel better, he'd gladly take the blame. He has yearned for the confrontation and prepared a levelheaded rebuttal to the charge. The truth is anything could cause pneumonia. Doctors agreed. And Torrance around so many dirty kids at school—who could blame him? It was just Max's time to go, that's all. It's sad, it sucks, it will always hurt, but it's over now. Pigeonholing the birds, the father reasoned, was a coping mechanism. Part of the grieving process. Once they were gone maybe she'd turn the crosshairs on him.

Torrance, at the wall, keeps circling the same spot well after it's clean.

The mother arrives home late. Dinner's cooling on the stove. The father has already made Torrance say his prayers. The boy has been allowed to nibble on a butterless roll.

"Ha," the mother says, entering the house and removing her shoes. "Who wants to guess how many I got?"

"You're late," the father says.

"Torrance?"

"Five?" Torrance asks.

"Oh, no."

"Do you need to gloat?"

"Eight?"

"Nope."

"Not a dozen," the father says.

"And it's only day one!" the mother exclaims.

"Any in flight?" Torrance asks.

"Nearly all of them. One flew away with my arrow."

"It's egregious," the father states.

"Hey, they're big birds. They don't have to come here and kill our children."

"Would you clean up for dinner?"

"Where are they?" Torrance asks.

"Wanda's got a full-size freezer in her garage. We're going to keep them in there until it's over. All told the MAC's took forty-two. We even beat the American Rifling Club. I think the only group who bagged more than us was the VFW. But they'll tire as the week goes on, mark my word."

"We're eating."

"I'll just be a sec," the mother says. She whistles into the bedroom.

The father ladles stew into bowls. Torrance swings his legs under the table and rubs his eye.

"Tell me about school, son," the father says.

Torrance doesn't want to talk about it.

"What are you learning?"

"I don't know."

"You've got to do better than that, Tory."

"They're studying state capitals," the mother says, returning to the kitchen. She's put her hair in a ponytail and slipped into a sweat suit.

"What else?"

"I don't know, Dad. I don't want to talk about it."

"Not good enough," the mother says.

"Mom."

"Look, I'm in a good mood. I'm happy. Don't blow it," the mother says through her up-turned lips. "Pass the rolls, Frank."

Reluctantly, Torrance says, "I'm worried about tomorrow."

"Why?" the father asks.

Torrance spoons his stew.

"Do you have a big test?" the mother asks. "Look at me when I speak to you."

"No."

"We can't read your mind," the father says.

"I can read his mind," the mother contradicts. "It's all cloudy tonight. What's the prognosis, doctor?"

Torrance finds it difficult to keep things from his mother. He feels like a marionette under her gaze. "Tomorrow is Scoliosis Day," he admits.

"Oh, don't worry about it," the father says. "Your spine's fine."

"How do you know?" the mother asks.

"Why wouldn't it be?"

"Sit up, Torrance. Keep your back straight. You slouch too much, like your father."

The father sits up-right.

"It's not my spine I'm worried about," Torrance says.

"I've never noticed anything wrong with his spine, is all I'm saying," the father elaborates. "Slouching doesn't make it crooked, anyhow."

"Stand up," the mother gestures with a hand. "Take your shirt off and turn around."

"Mom!"

"Don't fight me," she insists.

"I don't want to take my shirt off."

"I'm your mother."

"Tomorrow. In front of everyone."

"Don't be silly," the father says. "Guys go shirtless all the time."

"I just don't."

"Practice now, in front of us."

"Mom, I don't want to."

"Just close your eyes, it won't hurt," the mother softly hums.

"Max told me about it. He said it was horrible. Kids teased him. They said he looked like a bag of sticks and stones."

The mother purses her lips.

"All right," the father says. "I see what this is about."

"What is it about?" the mother says, swiveling.

"Dear, this is a hard time for all of us."

"Hard time?"

"I caught Torrance in the cemetery this afternoon."

Torrance feels the constriction in his throat relax and surprise pop across his brow.

"Torrance?" the mother asks.

"I told him I wouldn't tell you—he didn't want to get in trouble for leaving the yard."

"You went to see Max?"

"Don't push him, Hun."

"How do you think he came into this world?"

"Don't rush, now," the father coaxes. "Tory, I'll call the school nurse tomorrow and get her to view you in private. Your brother was sick, but he was strong. He was better than them, not made for this world. Everything here was beneath him. Don't forget that."

"That's true," the mother agrees, leaning back in her chair with her eyebrows arched. "Now eat."

Torrance is wearing his brother's jacket. It's a little tight, but more appropriate for the temperature. He hops off the last step of the bus and onto the pavement. His backpack is lighter than usual this afternoon—the teacher, a crow hunter, was in good spirits and decided on little homework. Just memorize a half-dozen mid-western rivers.

The clouds are hogging the sky. Torrance can't remember when he last saw the sun. The gray makes sense to the boy; it's all part of something big.

A crow in the neighbor's drive rolls a stone around in its beak and nods. Torrance nods back. They share a secret.

The mother is waiting with the other MAC's. Torrance takes his time walking up to them. He practices whistling as he comes. The flag on the pole is dying for attention.

"How did I let you get out of the house with that on this morning?" the mother asks.

"I don't know," Torrance answers.

"It's a nice jacket," Ruby's mother says.

"We could stitch a MAC's patch on it," the bruiser chips in.

"Don't," Torrance's mother hisses through her teeth. She cuts her eyes at the bruiser.

"I'm sorry," the woman says, with arms outstretched. "I just meant for support."

"This is Max's jacket."

"I know, Tory. It's not yours. Go inside and take it off."

"Can I play in the yard?"

"*May* I," a mother corrects.

"You going to stay in the yard?"

"May I go a little further?"

The mother stares hard at her boy. She has thought about this all day. Torrance hasn't done much in the way of grieving. She knows. She watches him closely. Going to the cemetery yesterday is big. Maybe he just needs a little room. And now the jacket.

"In a coat, maybe," the mother says.

———

Torrance removes his shoes and then uses the bathroom. From the window he watches the women leave. When they are gone, he removes a black magic marker from his backpack, slides into his shoes, and heads out. He keeps the jacket on. It is red and silver and has a hood for the wind.

Torrance walks by the cemetery and to the pumpkin field. From the jacket pocket he withdraws and unfolds a piece of worn paper. The page is filled with skeletons that Max drew. Max liked to draw. It is what he did to pass the time waiting to go to the hospital, while he was in the hospital, and when he was home recovering. Sometimes he'd show Torrance what he'd done. Many of the illustrations were really good. Torrance remembers one drawing of a snow-peaked mountain ringed by a halo of soft-white cloud. In the contours of the mountain there was supposed to be a face. Torrance pretended he could see it.

*When you look at that mound of trash out back, think of this picture*, Max had said. And Torrance tries.

Most of Max's things are boxed up in the attic and off limits. Keeping them hidden was the mother's idea so she can furtively rifle through them during the day when nobody is home.

But the jacket was over-looked in the back of the closet.

Torrance sprints across the field—a battlefield strewn with decapitated heads and occasional flaps of scalp—and to the big pumpkin. Withdrawing the magic marker, Torrance tries to copy the face of the scariest skeleton from the page onto the pumpkin. There are sharply angled eyebrows in the form of two flapping birds. The eyes are side-by-side scythe blades and the handles form the bridge of the nose. The mouth gapes in a frozen scream. Torrance sticks his tongue out as he tries to get the proportions right and when he's done he steps back to scrutinize his work. It's all wrong. Not even close, really. This pumpkin is not frightening at all. The nose is crooked, the mouth is an irregular circle, brows are too straight, and the eyes are more dumb than haunted. Torrance stamps his feet and swipes his chin. When he tries to smear the marker off the pumpkin, it won't come clean.

"Hell," he says. He spits defiantly with the wind. "Let me try this again."

Sizing up a pumpkin a few rows over, Torrance does his best to make what's on the page come alive. The mouth is better, but the nose is off. Forget about the eyes. He starts on a different pumpkin which is too soft, so he finds one still hard and sketches the face. This time, it's not bad. It's passable. On the page are a dozen different skeletons. Luckily, the skulls are bald and with the right hand could look fine on pumpkins. The paper in one hand and the marker in the other, Torrance sets to work capturing the expressions of Max's skeletons on the pumpkins. He moves from the back of the field forward.

By the time Torrance is startled by a car honking its horn from the county road, Torrance has decorated fifty or so pumpkins. Some of them are looking at the sky, others stare at the ground, and many regard each other.

"Excuse me," the woman in the car, a yellow Mazda, calls out.

Torrance holds his ground. "Ma'am?"

"Could you come over here?"

Torrance straightens. He cracks his neck, caps the marker, and folds the paper back into the jacket pocket.

"You lost?"

"Maybe," the woman says. "Could you help me?"

Torrance, curious, brushes dirt off his pants and steps tentatively over to the woman. She has red hair and green eyes and when she runs her tongue across the row of her upper teeth, Torrance is tantalized. He stands close enough to hold a conversation and far enough to bolt back into the field.

"My name is Cindy Sampson," the woman says, idling in the car. She waits a moment to see if this name registers.

"That sounds like candy."

Cindy's laugh is quick and twittering. "That's sweet to say. What were you doing out there?" When Cindy tosses her head to indicate the field, her hair shakes loose across her forehead.

Torrance doesn't want to explain this. "I've been told not to talk to strangers."

"Your Mom tell you that?"

Torrance holds his ground.

"Well," Cindy says, "you're a wise boy. But I've already told you my name. I work for the *Observer*. A writer. A reporter. I'm working on an article."

"For the newspaper?"

"Yes. I was told I could find members of the Mothers Against Crows around here."

Torrance notices black marker on his wrists. He tries to rub it away.

"The crows. You know about the crows?"

"Yeah," Torrance says.

"What do you know?"

"Well," the boy says, "a lot of people call a bunch of crows a 'murder,' I know that."

"Sure," Cindy says, "that is what they're called."

"My brother told me never to refer to them as a murder and never to trust anyone who does."

"I'll keep it out of my article."

"Ornithologists call them a flock."

"Maybe I could talk to you and your brother for the paper.

How are children being affected by the crows? There could be room. Would you like that?"

Torrance wrings his hands.

"I'll need your parent's permission. Where can I find them?"

The boy puckers his lips.

"What about your brother, then? Maybe he's eighteen?"

"He stays out of this."

"OK," Cindy says. She takes out a notepad. "Let's you and I see if we can work something out. What do you think about all the crows here in Auburn?"

"It's just part of the season. No matter where you live, everyone gets shit on by a bird once and a while," Torrance says. "There's no avoiding it. It's what a person does afterwards is what's important."

"I can't use *shit*," Cindy scribbles away, "although I like the local color."

"There are two kinds of people," Torrance continues, "those who wipe the stuff off every time and those that go and kill the bird."

"What do you believe people should do?"

"Nothing. I don't believe in nothing."

"That's a double negative. I can't use that. Plus it means that you believe in something…"

"It doesn't make a whit of difference what you do. You're just going to get dumped on again."

Torrance catches sight of the little cloud his father's sedan is creating as it hustles down the county road.

"Nice. They're part of the landscape. You've grown up with them. You don't even really see them, do you?"

"I see them. They might have killed my brother. He once told me that crows help dead people make the transition into the afterlife."

"Well, that's…"

"It's a myth," Torrance interrupts. "Ask that man."

Before Cindy can follow up the boy has spun away and lifted off.

Torrance swings his legs under the table and drags his socks along the floor. Tonight his mind is too full for dinner. He eats the dried fish because he understands the consequences of not eating.

The mother chews deliberately and steals glances at her boy often.

"Tell me about school, son," the father says.

"School, school, school, school," Torrance sings.

"Did you get tested?" the mother asks.

"Yup."

"And?"

"I'm clear. My spine's fine."

"See," the father says.

"And you took your shirt off?"

"Of course, Mom. I thought we had to do it in front of everyone, but we didn't. I stood behind a screen. I don't know what Max was talking about."

The mother pounces. "Did you go see him today?" she asks. "Look at me when we talk about him."

"Let's not, then."

"Did you go?" The mother's sharp voice snaps the boy's neck to her.

"Yes," Torrance says.

"Then you saw what I put there."

"Sure," Torrance says, with as much conviction as he can.

"Is anyone going to fill me in?" the father asks.

Torrance and the mother are silent—the mother in her smile and the boy with his lips puckered—both digesting the lie.

After a minute passes, the mother breaks the lock on her son. "You'll have to go and see yourself, dear."

"I'm intrigued."

Torrance asks if he can be excused.

"There was a reporter snooping around this afternoon—for the *Observer*. She's writing an article about the crows," the father says.

Torrance slumps further down his chair.

"Just what we need," the mother says.

"Asked about the MAC's."

"You tell her those birds killed my son?"

"Our boy. You know I wouldn't say that."

"What did you say?"

"The birds have a right to be here."

"Ha," the mother laughs.

"Everyone has a right to his opinion."

"Yours stink."

Torrance looks at the empty seat across from him and sees Tension sitting there toying with his broccoli.

"You want to talk about this?"

"Anytime, Frank. Talk, talk, talk, talk, talk."

The father's weak chin sags into his chest. The mother's back is so straight it's nearly bent backward. "Let's go around and around and around."

Tension rises from his chair. Torrance wants to follow. He takes a deep sigh and asks, "How many birds did you take tonight?"

———

It's raining when Torrance steps off the bus in a mood. He's draped in a rain slicker and the water bounces off his yellow hood and rolls down the covered backpack. Even mostly dry like he is, the boy is shivering. The cold has gotten under his skin.

Standing in the neighbor's driveway waiting under a black umbrella is Torrance's father. His frowning lips are weighing down his chin and the hat conceals his charcoal-colored eyes. Dwarfed beneath the wide umbrella and with his patient legs neatly tucked together, he looks foreboding to Torrance—a dark messenger.

Reluctantly, Torrance greets him. "Guess God's cleaning the church today?"

"Cute," the father says.

"Mom?"

"Rain doesn't kill the crows."

Father and son shuffle toward the house. When they're close enough, Torrance notices the absent flag. The father tries to keep his boy under the umbrella.

"I don't need that," Torrance says. "What happened to the flag?"

"Let's not go there. Tell me about school."

"I learned so much."

"You can always be somebody different than you are, son. I ask because I care. Do you know how much I care?"

"I think so," Torrance says, lowering his head and following the splattering rain's lead. "Then maybe you'll understand that there's something I've got to do."

"Shoot."

"I need to go to Max's grave."

"Tory, it's raining."

"I know. That's why I must go. To get what Mom left. It will get ruined."

The father stares down at the shape of his son's head under the slicker. "Fine. Let's go there now."

"I have to pee."

"Afterwards, then."

"Dad, please. This is something between me and Max and Mom." Torrance knows this isn't what his father wants to hear and he also knows that it is exactly what he should say.

The father is quiet the rest of the walk home. When they're on the porch, he says, "Put on different shoes."

Torrance leaves the house with a head of apprehension. He does not want to go to the cemetery and all the same he is dying to see what his mother left. More than anything he wants to wiggle his way out of the lie he slipped into last night. All day he's been wondering what she could have put next to Max's headstone. His fear and his best guess is that she put a sketch out there, something nice Max drew, and it's been falling apart since Torrance was called in early at recess. It could be something else. The mother is crafty. She quilts and sews and solders and can turn macaroni into figurines. Max used to like the silk flowers the mother made, so she made them by the dozen, and it tears Torrance up to think her roses are being punished in the weather.

At the same time, Torrance doesn't want to visit Max's grave. It's a place so close to the house that it shouldn't be a big deal. Ever since the burial, when the slim, slick, cherry wood coffin dropped down like a seed planted in front of the polished and blanched white headstone, Torrance has stayed away. He knows his parents go there regularly (the mother sometimes goes twice or more a day) to *commune* with Max—prayer from the father and a one-sided conversation from the mother—and while this may provide them with some degree of comfort Torrance can't imagine it doing anything for him. Torrance misses his brother. He's been gone nearly a year and most days Torrance asks himself what Max was doing exactly one year ago. Torrance has to make a lot of this up. One year ago today, Torrance knows, Max went to the movies with the mother and when Torrance came home from school, his brother told him all about it. Torrance can't recall the name of the film, but he remembers that it was rated R. Max said he couldn't understand why it was rated that way and Torrance couldn't understand why the mother would take him to that film.

The falling rain has tails. The sky is reluctant to let it go. It shoots out from the low clouds like thin arrows and stings Torrance's face. The snow boots he's got on make walking cumbersome. If he has to run, for any reason, he'll be slow and certainly get caught.

The grass of the cemetery is slippery. The boy picks his way through, cold to the bone, and weighted down by dread.

Max's grave is not nestled against other headstones. The mother purchased four plots; she already has dying planned out. Right now Max is alone. Someday this will change. When he arrives, Torrance surveys the grounds. He doesn't see anything other than a few stray leaves that have blown over from their backyard. Knowing his mother, Torrance realizes that he might need to kneel down and get a little dirty in order to discover what she left. Shaking, he takes a knee and steadies himself with his hands on the ground. He stays this way with his head bent just taking in breath and letting it out.

The name on the headstone reads *Maxwell* which seems off to Torrance since Max was never really well at all. Maybe in the afterworld the name makes more sense.

Torrance can't find what his mother left. There are no flowers and no drawings. It is possible that she came out here earlier today to retrieve it. Maybe she never put anything out here in the first place. Trying to think this through, Torrance hears, over the chanting rain, a faint clamoring sound. He cocks his head and strains to hear. It's something, that's for sure, and it may have been there all along.

Rising, Torrance startles a crow crouching behind a headstone that startles the boy with its sudden warning call. The two flinch and try to settle—shaking off the rain and regaining composure. At first, Torrance thinks the bird has been pecking at some dead animal. There's a pile of sinewy mush the crow has been feeding on. But it isn't a carcass, just pumpkin innards. Curious, Torrance approaches. The crow bounces a few feet back, spitting and hissing as it does, and crests on a leaning cross near the back of the cemetery. And then, Torrance sees another bird at another pile. And, yet another. He wearily follows, moving toward the sound, feeling as if he's done all this before.

The mounds of pumpkin lead Torrance to the edge of the cemetery and the tree line. He wades through brambles before he is released from the graveyard and in the field and there he is greeted by the cacophony of crow caws. In the field the pumpkins have been gutted and hundreds of crows are feasting on the flesh. The smell of the wet birds and the gore hit Torrance in a sour-tasting wave. Among the triangular bird tracks imprinting the mud are many footprints as if an army has crossed. Torrance knows that it wasn't an army. He can clearly see what's happened here.

All the faces that he drew on yesterday have been hastily carved into the pumpkins. The jack-o'-lanterns sit beside their brains accompanied by the crows. And there they wail at each other in agony and in celebration.

# MINUTE MINUTE

The cuckoo in the clock is damaged and the chimes have rusted so that on the hour, when the door drops and the bird is supposed to burst out and call, there's only a grinding noise like chewing a mouthful of salt and no twittering fowl. The wooden pendulum swings and ticks and tries to shrug off the dust. Needle watches and breathes in time. There is a newspaper spread across his lap and a cup of lukewarm coffee next to the sofa he's sitting upon. Outside the front window Needle's father breaks from the lingering morning fog as he shuffles to the porch steps and the door.

Needle's father delivers newspapers. It's a kind of penitence for abandoning his wife. He first learned of her passing three pages deep in the *Examiner*. She slipped and tumbled, kept tumbling, down an upward-moving escalator at the mall. Paps was at the cabin with poker buddies sequestered but for the Sunday paper. That was nine years ago. Now he's eighty and fit and not in the mood to argue. He can go all day and never get winded. He claims there is an art to walking. He is a paperman; not boy. He enters the house with his sacks swinging empty and a few droplets of sweat beading at his hairline.

"Neighborhood's abuzz," Paps says.

Needle flinches and looks down at his hand to where his index finger is pointing, like it has been waiting, at the front-page story.

Paps slumps into the recliner across from Needle and wipes his brow with an age-speckled forearm. "About whether he jumped or fell."

Needle makes a fist, uncrosses his legs and folds the paper. "Paper insinuates he jumped."

"Exactly," Paps says.

Needle takes a sip of his coffee and lets it linger in his mouth a moment before swallowing. When it's down, he says, "You remember what color that bird is?"

"Blue. Or brown," Paps replies. "You all right, Needy?"

"Like eyes."

"I spoke with Jenny, paid my condolences, inquired about calling hours."

"How is she?" Needle asks.

"It's too soon. She doesn't know them yet. She said there was no note..."

"He wouldn't do that."

"...and that he was fine," Paps continues. "Acting normal. At dinner he talked about shingling the roof."

Paps scrutinizes his son in a gathering pause before saying, reproachfully, "If you have any reason to believe something was off, you better come clean with it. Jen has a right to know."

"People are going to believe what they want to believe."

"Still, whatever comfort can be found comes from friends and family. It's no solution. God knows. I carry your mother around every day. But my heart's an obstreperous thing." Paps uses two fingers to tap his chest. "Not yours, huh, son?"

"I miss Mom, too," Needle whispers.

Paps doesn't hear this clearly. He's not the kind of man who gives up easily. "So, you think he jumped or fell?"

Needle catches the breath in his throat and chokes a little. When he tries to speak the clock grinds out the words.

It is easy for Needle to pack up his bedroom. He fills a duffle bag with clothes, a suitcase with bed linen and toiletries, and a backpack with a tarnished trophy, a photograph, a deck of cards, and a length of rope. He slips a newspaper cutout under the rubber band at his wrist, pulls the blinds, and leaves the room, the house.

Paps, in the garage stuffing newspapers into thin orange plastic sleeves, watches his son go.

When the muscles in his arm burn from the weight Needle swings the bags and loosens his grip. He moves from the kind of neighborhood where people give someone swinging bags a wide berth to the kind of neighborhood where people purpose-fully bump into them.

Needle steps around a loud trio of loiterers huddled near the remnants of a park bench. Shrug off taunts and move the suitcase from right hand to left and the duffle from left to right, without slowing.

An acorn falls from a tree and pops against a fire hydrant then into the tall grass. Cars made mostly of stereos and speak-ers negotiate tight, pot-hole pocked roads. The sun takes a few steps into a blind alley. Buildings lean forward and try to in-timidate each other. Note the missing bricks, broken glass, and dented gutters. The sidewalk is fragmented and often stained.

Needle's footfalls are high and steady. He glances at street signs and the horizon—smokecloud yellow-gray factory heave—power lines like gradients providing space for what is otherwise nothing. The sidewalk gives up to a concrete expanse punctuated with drainage ditches for sky runoff and leaks.

A blue van with a smiling sandwich painted on its side, the mobile lunch vendor, hurries past Needle to set up where anyone can see it. The driver, a quick man from Burma, slides out tables, snaps open an umbrella, displays hoagies, hamburgers, chips, and coolers packed with drinks. He rattles wind chimes affixed to the rear van door.

Needle buys a dog, which the vendor zaps in a battery-powered microwave, and a drink and sits next to an orange cone just as employees trickle out.

There is an unspoken order to lunch. First come the foremen and navy-blue suits that do not have time to wait. They watch their watches, order tuna sandwiches and chips and leave bills in the plastic pickle tip jar. Because they have desks, they'll eat at them.

Next are the receptionists and administrators who claim a park bench beneath a cluster of tough elm. They buy bottled water and dig into salads and energy bars they've brought from home.

Lastly come the high-beam-walking grunts who wear smudged hardhats and tar-stained blue jeans. Today, cinched around their arms are black bands, a kind of tribute to Lester Noone. The skin around their eyes is clean and soft, protected by goggles; the rest of their faces look like peanut butter. They let their arms dangle loosely and talk sporadically at one another. They clean the vendor out and congregate in patches of weeds near the picnic bench or anywhere else, appreciating the ground.

The vendor clicks on the van radio and hikes it up. A classic rock song ends with a screaming guitar solo and then an excited announcer shouts out the details of *Monster Truck Madness* tonight and *Motocross Mayhem* tomorrow at the Pit. Two men sprawl beside the orange cone, like they own it, and nod at Needle who is staring up at the scaffolding of an unfinished building. The men are immortally young with squinting eyes and easy grins. They finish their food before Needle swallows the last of his hot dog bun.

One of the men reclines on the cone and sets his hardhat over his face. The other man runs his upper lip across the bottom row of his teeth and picks at a scab at his elbow. To Needle, after a while, he says, "You looking for work?"

Needle retired two years ago to watch over his father who doesn't need watching over. "What's it like up there?"

"It's not like anything," the man with the scab says.

"Like dancing with birds," the other man offers.

"They give you a harness if you're worried about falling."

"Not everyone uses it."

A jet is dividing the sky with contrails above. "How far can you see?" Needle asks.

"Depends on which way you look," the man with the scab answers. "They tell you not to look down, but that's plain dumb. Just imagine the ground is *right there*, a foot away. Then get the job done."

"Sometimes I can see the ocean," the other man mumbles into his hardhat.

"In your dreams, Dan. Hey," the man with the scab says to Needle, "you mind if I rest a while on your bag? Looks soft."

Needle doesn't resist. The man emits a hoot and settles onto the duffle for a quick nap.

Dan sits up and sets the cone and hat aside, flashes a skyward smile. "You let me borrow that backpack and I'll put in a word for you. My word's good, honest."

Where the industrial park ends, Eastside begins. Needle walks right past the bus station, his bags swinging at his sides. It is afternoon now and without the factory cloudsmoke the sun can pitch Needle's silhouette out in front of him. Needle's just shy of six feet but is ten-foot tall in shadow. His head is a balloon and his arms, with the bags, look like wings.

Beyond the bus station is a hardware store nestled between a pair of bars. Except for the different neon beer signs in the windows, the places are identical. Drinkers inside don't bother turning as Needle trudges by.

Railroad tracks slither out of the center of town and pace the road Needle walks along. Things quite suddenly become rural. A tired neighborhood rolls into the farmland fringe. Houses here populate their porches with dolled-up ceramic geese. Flags on poles hang in the windlessness. Needle is followed by the sound of rusty screened doors opening as unoccupied Eastsiders rubberneck.

Stop at the house with the lawn covered in kitsch. Everything—workman's boots, a high chair, a tractor tire, rakes, mittens, overalls, sketches of boats, a bed frame, a set of incomplete encyclopedias, brown-rimmed dishes, a small animal cage, baseball caps, a mirror ball, matchbox cars, stools, posters, Christmas ornaments, other trinkets—has a yellow sticker with a price scribbled on it. Puddles of water stand in the contours of a blue tarp heaped by a pine. Needle drops his bags and picks up a boot. He checks the size.

A broad woman with a straw hat and a mason jar in her hands pushes out from the house and hurries down the porch steps to greet Needle.

"Those boots are in good shape," she says, brushing a clump of dirty-yellow hair off her face.

"Whose were they?" Needle asks.

"Everything's negotiable."

"They're too big," Needle says, setting the boot back with its match. He double checks the underside of his wrist where he slipped the *Room for Rent* newspaper clipping. "You Minnie?"

"I am," she says, trying to see what Needle's got there.

"You still have a room?"

"Sure do. My boy's old place behind the house. It's nothing fancy."

"May I see it?"

Take the room which occupies the ground floor of a small barn. Convince Minnie to rent it week-by-week. Let her hem and haw about such a short period of time. Wonder why looking at the ceiling changes her mind to say, *On second thought...*

The door to the loft is padlocked. Smells like gasoline and hay. Find the room furnished with old, listless apartment stuff—a bed, a chest, a lamp, a bathroom rug, a toaster oven, and a mirror (don't look, you know how you appear). There is a checkered flag tacked on the wall over the twin frame. The cheap linoleum floor is cracking in places. It is quiet. The door to the closet has a fist-hole indenting it.

On the bedside table Needle sets his tarnished trophy. In high school he was on the winning baseball team. He once got an important hit. Atop four brass columns a figurine stands ready to swing at an imaginary pitch. The bat is chipped and looks more like a wand; the minute man a baffled magician.

Just outside are bird bones like toothpicks by the front door. Ants have made a mound in proximity. The railroad tracks are about fifty yards from Needle's front door. Minnie insists trains don't run much after midnight. There are piles of railroad ties, where hornets nest, just on the other side of the tracks. Next to the barn are the remains of a beat up stock car, number 316 painted black on the sides—orange tendrils of flame on the roof. The front end has been accordianed; the hood is neatly folded like in prayer. Wild patches of mint have grown up around the wheel wells.

Evenings Minnie sits in a rocking chair with a drink and watches the long sunset stretch the horizon. A patchy wheat field rustles nervously as if it is concealing something. Beneath a line of trees in the distance is a silo.

"I got another rocker in the front yard," Minnie says when Needle approaches to stand at her side. "I'll fetch it for you. Drink?"

"No," Needle answers. Just sit on the grass. The yard has been recently mowed.

"I appreciate the company," Minnie says, rocking.

Needle appreciates it too. It's one day nearly done.

"Family?" Minnie asks.

"My father, still."

"No children?"

"Nothing like that, no."

"Job?"

"Retired plumber."

"That's good, sometimes the faucet sticks."

A heavy cat jumps out of the car window and crosses the tracks on its way to the old lumber.

"That belong to you?" Needle asks.

"She's my boy's. Sixpack. Got six digits on each paw."

"316's an odd number."

Minnie hikes her skirt to get at a mosquito bite. There are scars on her calves. "That's my boy's too," she says lowly with her chin to neck.

"I don't mean to pry," Needle says.

"What's there to say?" Grass around the rocking chair is longer; the mower didn't bother to move it. "It's in reference to John. I don't know why I keep it. Either I'm sentimental or just plain morbid."

Needle knows the story. Minnie's son Cooper survived the first accident but not the second one. "Maybe you're not ready to let go."

Minnie mumbles into her drink. Needle fiddles with his hands. After a while Minnie asks, "Are you prepared?"

Needle stretches his legs forward and loosely massages them. "I'm not sure."

"Watch the rail."

The tracks vibrate and a bit of gravel trickles down the small rise.

"It's almost eight."

A tiny light faintly appears where the railroad tracks seem to come to a point. Eventually Needle makes out a drifting plume of smoke and the trainface. And then there is sound. It hits the gut first and then rattles the heart as the head makes sense of it. There's not much time to think before it is passing. One steel wave tumbling forward. What it's made of—weights and pulleys, measured cars carrying graffiti, passengers in motion—is not much more than an impression. Question the details, but not the impact of it having been here, as it moves away.

"Whoosh," Minnie says, draining her drink.

Night arrives, as if the train is pulling the sun along, in the wake of the machine.

"Hold it now," Minnie says poising a finger in the air. "Hear that silence?"

Needle strains to listen for nothing in the fade of the roar.

"Ten, nine, eight," Minnie counts, "seven, six..."

"What?"

"Crickets. Like clockwork. They take their cue from the train. Rise up."

The insects make enormous noise, all at once.

"My entertainment," Minnie says. "And it's not over yet. You have my seat. I've got to pull a few of the better items out front into the garage. Should you need anything tonight, ring the bell."

Minnie rocks herself to her feet and walks heel-to-toe in her flip-flops through the lawn. Her skirt is crooked and her blouse half-tucked. She tugs at it as she passes the cucumber garden growing up alongside the house.

Needle stays in the grass. Bats cut across the sky. A dome of light from fifty halogen-trees illuminates the night some miles down the tracks at the Pit. Soon the voice of an announcer overcomes the buzzing backdrop. Needle can't make out words, but he recognizes the pitch changes as the commentator tries to drum up excitement and expectation from the crowd. Truck engines boom and the tinny explosion of cheer and applause erupts.


Midday Needle hears a ping and a thud. He whittled away the morning over a newspaper he picked up from the dispenser at the corner. The drive-in movie theatre has midnight showings of *Into the Howlers, Fidget,* and *Heart Ripples.* They need an attendant at the gas station. There was a drug-related stabbing. These are Garage Sale days. The baseball team is struggling. Several angry letters have been written to the editor. People are furious at the journalist who implied Lester Noone jumped. The letters list reasons he wouldn't and insist, *No way.* On the back page is a picture of Lester with a brief bio. The weather will be clear and mild. Tonight is a quarter moon.

Needle opens the front door to investigate. See Sixpack hunched down and ready to pounce. A stunned bird tries to chirp. Sixpack is on it and away around the corner of the barn. A few brown feathers hang in the air like a second-thought. Needle closes the door and sits down at the edge of the bed.

The newspaper picture doesn't look right to Needle since it is black and white. One first notices the color of Lester's eyes. Nearly yellow in a jaundiced way. Here they are just black. In the shot his beard is neatly trimmed and his mouth half-open as if he is saying "cheese" for the photographer. His hair is plastered down over his ears, like he just removed a helmet; Lester had several helmets—the construction kind, a fireman's (he volunteered), and one for his motorcycle. Needle can't tell if the picture was taken inside or outside, the background is just too dark. Stretching to his duffle, Needle withdraws the picture he carries and places it in his lap next to the newspaper shot.

The Chicago skyline dominates Needle's picture—breathtaking and expansive. Lester's young face is out of focus and blurry in the bottom corner of the frame. He's got his head thrown back to the camera as his body moves toward the railing.

In fifth grade Needle's elementary school class took a field trip to the Sears Tower. When Needle asked his Dad for souvenir money, Paps dug out his old camera and warned his boy to take care. The highlight of the trip was atop the Tower in the circular observation deck where kids could see as much of the world as they could imagine. Lester wanted more. While Mrs. Raurbach led the wide-eyed others around, Lester and Needle tip-toed back to the elevator, took it down to the highest office building, an architecture firm, and snuck through the quiet lunchtime floor to the deserted corner office with a balcony. Think back on it now, question how easy it had all been. Then, though, Needle knew the world worked the way Lester wanted it to work. Bad things always skimmed over Les; he was like a lone stick of grass pardoned by the blade. So Needle stayed close. It made sense that they should find themselves slinking toward a chest-high wrought-iron railing claiming all that they surveyed—Chicago with its shoulder-pads and split-lip beauty. It was something to remember. And in an instant, when the building actually *swayed* (that's why Lester isn't centered in the photograph, Needle stumbled as he clicked), their lives changed. Needle has thought hard about the moment, stared long at the picture, and each time tries to find something— the shape of a cloud, a message in the windows of a distant building, the black speck that could be a bird or a flaw in the development—he might have missed that forecasts their fate unfolding.

"You feel that?" Lester asked, having made it to the rail.

Needle, on puppet strings, approached and looked down. He felt the weight of the camera strapped around his neck and worried about it momentarily. They stood still and willed, apprehensively, the building to move again so they could be sure it wasn't their imagination the first time.

Through the remove of years Needle has often wondered who had the desire first or if, the way things are sometimes, the thought was conceived in the same moment.

"Hey, Needy," Les whispered, "I've got this crazy urge to jump. You know what I mean?"

That urge paralyzed Needle. He visualized throwing his leg over the rail and rolling himself out into the air. It wasn't that he wanted to die, and in the back of his mind he knew there was only death below, the yearning was deep and urgent; a craving to experience the sensation of falling.

The skyline disappeared as Needle tried to focus on the ground. He saw street-shade black and a strip of concrete-colored sidewalk. Then his straining vision faltered, the blood rushed to his head, a flock of pins tingled across his chest and out to the tips of his fingers and for an instant—like a long blink—he fainted.

When Needle regained his balance he glanced over and saw Lester standing on the outside of the rail leaning back, looking down, and holding on with just one hand.

"What the fuck?" Needle said and in the swearing, something he rarely did, he mustered the courage to hurry over, grab Lester's arm, and yank him close enough to hug.

"Got me?" Les said, closing his eyes, going limp, relaxing his body, dangling his feet. Later Les would try to laugh it all off—*I knew you wouldn't let me go.*

Needle stared straight ahead, too afraid to look down now, and struggled to find his strength. Although Lester was bigger than Needle, adrenaline overpowered dead weight and the two collapsed back on the weather-beaten balcony floor.


With her drink in one hand, Minnie pulls a rocking chair from the front lawn around back for Needle. He takes it quietly.

"Drink?" Minnie asks.

"No, I don't think so," Needle replies.

"You have a problem with it?"

"Not me. It's in my blood, though."

Minnie flares her nostrils and takes air in loudly. "Blood, huh? My boy had his father's blood. Unfortunately, his father was a fool," she rolls her eyes. "Tired of me, I suppose. I don't blame him for that—I won't roll over easily. One night, probably a night I made him sleep down on the couch, he heard

a train passing and decided to chase after it. Gone like that."
Minnie snaps her fingers. "Bye, bye, mister."

"Cooper try to run away?" Needle asks, withdrawing a
length of rope from his pocket.

Minnie puts a thick hand on Needle's thin arm. "I never
told you my boy's name."

Pulling away, Needle threads one end of the rope through a
double loop and pulls. "I read the papers."

"Seems to me you think you know something."

"Oh, not much, really," Needle says, tugging at the knot.

"I suspect you ought to tell me," Minnie says, swiping the
rope from Needle's hands, "or I'll send you packing."

Needle folds his hands in his lap. "Well, a little over two
years ago, at the Pit, part of the *Doomsday Demo* series, your
boy Cooper was out crashing cars with all the rest."

Minnie drapes the rope over her shoulder, her face tight.

"He got rear-ended and spun around and knocked out. The
hazard crew was slow to react because it looked like no big deal.
No one saw the nest of flames breathing under the hood."

"Paper wasn't that thorough."

"The fire crept under and then inside the car and was sniffing around for the gasoline tank. That's when my pal Lester
acted. He scaled the retaining fence, dodged the traffic, sprint-
ed over and yanked your boy out. Then it exploded. They both
caught fire. Cooper was unconscious so he didn't feel it, I imagine. Les felt it right then and there and told me about it later.
He burned his hands so badly the fingernails fell off and never
came back."

Minnie leans forward and bunches her shirt up. "I never
knew who he was. By the time I got to the hospital..."

"Oh, well, yeah. He wouldn't have wanted that."

"Where can I find him?"

"I thought you should know, is all."

"That's why you came here?"

"His funeral is tomorrow."

Minnie stops rocking, her lips slightly parted. She looks down at her feet. Then she offers condolences that Needle cannot hear—the train arrives, passes. Afterwards, a pause. Then the uproarious bugs.

A camp of bats burst out of the silo. Needle says, "A bird collided with that window and the cat got it."

"Those are barn swallows. Before we converted it to Cooper's apartment they nested up there. When they first started banging off the glass my boy was convinced that they were trying to get back home. He opened the window and invited them inside. They didn't come. They only want to attack their own images. They have tiny brains. Saves me from buying cat food."

The lights from the Pit pop on. Soon, the announcer introduces tonight's event: *Motocross Mayhem*. Motorcycle engines whine. Crowd din follows.

"Les said the car was blue," Needle says, "with menacing clouds on the hood. Sky blew up."

"That was for demolition. He bought that stock car with his accident money. I thought the flames were morbid." Minnie offers the rope back to Needle. "Your friend did a good thing. Gave me more than I've come to expect from a man. Two years, three and a half months."

A quarter moon crests. Minnie stands and dumps her drink out by the tracks before excusing herself to head inside.

The railroad ties are too close together to take regular strides so Needle has to make miniature steps down the line. He watches his feet and tries not to turn an ankle. The ground to either side of the track is sloped and occasionally covered in brush. Underthings scamper. A tethered dog sounds like it has the hiccups. The junkyard fence picks up—high and wooden. Someone has tunneled under the slats and left a burrowed hole. Ahead of Needle, yards from the rail, a group of people huddle around a meek fire. They are engaged in a low conversation and don't take much notice of Needle.

The Eastside station stands a half-mile from where the fence ends. From there it is a short walk to the Pit. By the time Needle arrives at the gate, *Motocross Mayhem* is nearly complete. The announcer's voice is scratchy. Clusters of young men and women—at the tail end of beautiful—spill out of the speedway to smoke cigarettes and swear loudly. Those who came by train wait for those that drove to filter into the parking lot. Those that drove take their time, knowing this. Eventually everyone piles into a pickup or van or convertible—vehicles that are important—and hit *Sandy's* diner before the midnight showings at the drive-in.

Needle loops his fingers on the chain-link fence enclosing the Pit. Dirt kicked up by the shuffling crowd blooms in fields of light from halogen-trees. The snack shack shuts down. Tired racers wearing colorful shirts pull off their helmets, walk their mud-smeared motorcycles into hitched trailers, and then slump passenger side into leased wide-bodied pickups to be driven by a friend or a brother or a manager out the back way to the hotel up the road or home. Needle can't distinguish the winners from the losers.

The on-call ambulance exits.

Because the drive-in and the Pit are owned by the same woman, the lights go out before midnight. Needle's eyes take a moment to adjust. A pack of custodians collect all the trash

they can see. They make sure the couples who stayed to copu-
late in the bleachers have gone away before locking up and
heading to the bars. One cleaner eyes Needle propped against
the fence—drunks have done this before—and waits a minute
to see what kind of mess Needle will leave.

When Needle read in the paper (a blip buried in the sports
section), that Cooper was racing again, he told Les. Les never
wanted anything in return for saving Cooper's life; never con-
tacted the boy or Minnie. He shrugged off the *hero* label and
fought hard to stay out of the papers. After he learned about
the stock car, though, he returned to the Pit to see Cooper run.
And Cooper was good. The paper said he *drove fearlessly*. Les
carried a stop watch and timed laps. While other cars deceler-
ated into the turns, Cooper pushed harder and often won.

After a race sometime late last fall, Les introduced himself
to Cooper. The boy, sweaty in his suit and light-headed without the helmet, started in with his gratitude. Les cut him short,
they split a twelve pack back at Cooper's apartment, and Les
explained what he'd like as compensation.

Since he was a local and had a relationship with the Pit's
owner, Cooper carried a set of keys to the side-gate. That night,
well after midnight, Les strapped himself in passenger side and
convinced Cooper to drive without headlights around and
around the track, taking the banked-turns high.

Now, Needle coughs lightly. Thinking this is good enough,
the custodians speed off. The parking lot is empty except for a
pair of raccoons advancing.


Follow the tracks again and there are trees. The forest offers its
own kind of darkness. Inside is the irrelevance of time. Note

the infinity of leaves. Earth-smell and limb-lean. A brackish wet. The rhubarb hue.

Dirt paths beaten down by bikes bend through. Needle takes one. He holds an arm out in front of him, like he's bracing for a fall, and brushes away cobwebs and slim branches. He fords a sleepwalking creek and gets his shoes muddy. There are bumps along the trail and tire-tracks score the ground. Then, without ceremony, the path ends. The woods crowd together and squeeze the air out of Needle's lungs. Vines object. Bugs find skin and bite. Direction is meaningless—there's only ahead. Needle knows what lost feels like so he doesn't panic.

The woods consent abruptly. Needle pitches forward and collapses to his knees in a light-glow. For a moment the flickering husks before him look like grazing animals. Then a horn blares and another follows and the countenance of cars parked alongside speaker-posts makes Needle blink once and then crane his head up at the enormous movie screen he is beneath. In the film two men with guns are shouting at one another. This is the climax. Someone flashes high beams. Staying low to the ground Needle humps along the tree line until he is no longer in the way.

There are two other movie screens; one is rolling credits. Straightening, Needle cuts through an abandoned stretch of field. Follow a graveled road to the closed concession stand. The smell of popcorn lingers. Featured Pit events on faded flyers are tacked to the sides of the self-standing structure. A coiled hose drips. The wooden ladder rests against the back of the stand where it is out of the way.

Where the gravel meets pavement, the entrance and exit, is the movie signboard—a four-by four placard sitting atop two metal, fifteen foot posts. The movies are announced in black and capital letters which slide into tracks. The sign is backlit by twenty neon bulbs. A two-by-four has been secured between the posts so an employee can stand up there and make changes.

Needle props the ladder and steps back, a hand to his chin, to scrutinize the sign. The other movies end. Cars drive by. Some kids spit at him. Climb the ladder. Throw a leg over and clutch the post. Let the ladder clatter to the ground. Find balance and rise carefully.

A pickup with a bed full of high school band members pulls off the roadway to check this out. A trombone player suggests someone reposition the ladder. The flutist says to hang on a minute.

Needle splays his feet out to fit on the two-by-four and leans forward. A cloud of moths flutter. Other vehicles pull over to watch. A man in cut-offs tosses Milk Duds.

With all of his concentration, Needle begins to slide letters off the sign and re-arrange them. What he doesn't need, he throws aside. The on-lookers below wait. Everyone was disappointed by the way the movies ended. Everyone knew the last camera shot would cut from the embracing survivors, pan to the sky, and then fadeout. Everybody hopes for something better to happen here, now.

It takes a few minutes to spell, but Needle gets it right:

**LES**
**I FEEL IT TOO**
**RIP**

In the bed a tuba player scoffs. "Feel this, buddy," he says loudly, groping. Others, confused and unsatisfied, laugh. Then they are surprised to see Needle push himself off into empty space and drop.

———

Trains sound differently in the daytime. It's just intrusive noise. On his stomach, back in the apartment (the band members who felt badly hauled him home last night); Needle feels the vibration on the bed. The padlock to the loft above rattles.

Instead of sleeping, since he was dropped off last night, Needle has been tying knots. It is a way to occupy his hands. He knows: slip, running, anchor, overhand, figure eight, wall, timber, bowline, surgeon's, builder's, cat's paw, fisherman's bend, sheepshank, granny, half hitch, heaving-line, lanyard, noose loop, Matthew Walker; others. His tailbone is bruised badly but not broken. The quick fall wasn't what Needle had hoped for. He wanted more sensation. The better part of the thrill was standing up there hugging the sign and trying not to look down.

Shortly after the train passes, there is a ping-sound at the window. Later in the afternoon, as he paints his face with shaving cream, Needle hears a second collision. As someone outside cranks up a lawnmower, there is another loud bop and flutter. Needle pictures a parade of swallows bouncing off the window above to lie like a feast in the grass.

Outside a man in his late twenties is pushing a mower in diagonal strips across the backyard. The grass does not need this. Needle watches, not sure what else to do, until the man finishes. Needle will not buy a newspaper today. It isn't easy for him to fill the void without it. To kill time, he stands on the bed and inspects the padlock. When he hears tapping at the window he doesn't expect to see Minnie pressed to the glass and gesturing.

Step down, open the door and see what's the matter.

"There's nothing up there for you to see," Minnie hisses shaking her head so hard her black wide-brimmed hat slips. "I wish you'd stop snooping."

Before Needle has a chance to offer an explanation Minnie swivels, kicking up feathers, and marches in her funeral dress into the house.

Needle shuts the door quietly and stands in the corner where he can contemplate leaving. He is not exactly sure why he came here, but it wasn't to cause trouble. Needle has never been the kind of man who knows how to handle sorrow. In the aftermath of his mother's death, among the throng of supporters and well-wishers, Needle capitulated. While Paps cried and leaned on cousins and friends, drank with the poker buddies, Needle surrendered on the couch in the living room, ice melting in his lemonade, and was only coaxed up and out with force from Les. The two went bowling and crashed the pins.

Months ago Needle saw the *Room for Rent* ad and realized, after asking Les to remember where Cooper lived, that Minnie was the mother. Needle wondered about her loneliness—how it must feel to cope with nearly losing someone, and then really losing them. He suggested they pay a visit. The vacant room was a cry for help.

Les said to leave well enough alone.

Now Needle thinks maybe Les was right. Minnie's fine. She gets by—makes a little money in her front yard and keeps her nights occupied in the back yard. Time passes in between.

When Minnie steps outside with her drink, Needle is ready. He hustles to her side before she has a chance to settle in.

"I'm sorry," Needle says, winded. "About everything. Mostly, though, about your boy. I should have told you sooner."

Minnie, who has changed out of her dark clothes and slipped into sweat pants and a tee, is caught off guard. She spills her drink on her shirtfront. "Well," she says, "I didn't expect all this. Why don't you have a seat, you're making me nervous."

"I can't," Needle says. "I'll just stand here, if that's all right."

"Suit yourself," Minnie swats at a mosquito hovering at her hip. "I'm sorry for your loss, too."

"No, no…" Needle replies.

"Oh, yes. I went to his funeral today. He must have been well liked. There were tons of people."

It is less painful for Needle to lean forward.

"You didn't tell me it was a suicide," Minnie says.

Needle clasps his hands behind his back.

"I overheard a group of young women whispering."

"It's really not important," Needle tries to cut her short.

"Don't I know it," Minnie says, adjusting. "At Cooper's funeral there were young Pit people whispering, too. They said he must have had a *death wish*. He should have quit while he was ahead."

Needle senses momentum in Minnie's voice.

"You tell me why someone would go do again the thing that nearly killed him in the first place?"

"Well," Needle begins.

"Because you're a fool, that's why. Just like his father. He would have been better off hopping a train."

There's more color to Minnie's eyes when they are wet.

"God knows what kind of demons your friend was battling, but deep down he must have been beautiful to do what he did for Coop. My boy should have been there today on his knees and thankful." Minnie wipes away running mascara with her fingers. "Don't mind my crying. It comes and goes." Needle unfastens his hands from behind his back and rests one on Minnie's spine where it is exposed at the back of the neck.

"Aren't we quite a pair," Minnie says, craning her eyes, so the red vines are exposed, up at Needle. "I'll be all right in a minute."

"Let me get you a tissue," Needle says.

"I don't need one. I dry up quick," Minnie says, forcing a smile. "At least I get free lawn service. The young man who was involved in my son's accident comes by twice a week to mow," Minnie laughs in a deep burst. "Isn't that something?"

Needle keeps still, his brow furrowed, lips tucked; unblinking. A bit of papery snakeskin drifts by the rail. Faintly, in the distance, the tune from an ice cream truck plays.

"Thanks for listening to me," Minnie says as Needle steps out in front of her. "I apologize for acting so crazy this afternoon. Friends?" Minnie extends her hand.

"Sure," Needle replies, shaking mostly with his fingers.

There is a loose railroad spike standing higher than the others.

"You play cards?" Needle asks producing a deck from his back pocket.

"Solitaire," Minnie admits.

"Gin?"

"I drink plenty of it. Does that help?"

"Let's see," Needle says, handling the cards.

"I'm rusty."

"Let me explain."

Needle explains. Minnie remembers. She shuffles and deals and sets the pile in her ample lap. Needle stands bent and regards his cards with one hand at his chin. What's left of the sun finds Needle's eyes so that he screws up his face. Minnie makes a comment whenever Needle discards. She finishes her drink and could use another one. Needle notices that she pinches her knee every time she's about to go out. She beats Needle time and time again. All at once, she says, "I hope you never leave!"

Needle snatches a five of diamonds from Minnie's lap, something he'd been waiting for.

"That tickles," Minnie sputters, laughing staccato and overturning half the deck onto the ground. Needle feigns bending as if he could pick them up. Minnie gets them herself, offering Needle a peek at what she has.

Then the train, the bugs, the bats, the light and boom in the distance.

"We can finish this inside," Minnie presents, fluttering her eyelashes.

"I don't know," Needle hesitates.

"I've got a cold compress. It will help."


Needle wakes, contorted, in the stuffy dining room on Minnie's couch. His entire body is in pain. He can hear her softly snoring upstairs. A clock made out of a plate suggests it is early still. He rises with difficulty, finds the kitchen, and drinks tap water out of a frosted glass.

Everything in the kitchen is decorated with pigs—coffee cups, the toaster, towels, oven mitts, salt and pepper shakers, napkins, magnets on the refrigerator; most of them are smiling.

Look for aspirin in the junk drawer. Inside find scissors and tape, birthday candles, matches, scraps of loose paper. There's a small key hanging from a hook extending out of a pig snout above the sink. Forget the pain, grab the key, scissors, tape, and try to close the loud back door quietly.

Sixpack's swatting a cucumber on the vine.

Back in his apartment, Needle takes the checkered flag off the wall and, imagining what they look like, snips the fabric into the shape of a hawk. The head is not right, but the wings are impressive. Standing on the bed, he reaches the padlocked

door to the loft and inserts the key. There's an accordion ladder
on the underside of the hatch which Needle unfolds. Climbing
isn't easy on the back.

The loft is warm and blindingly-bright and rich with the
scent of wood from the interlocking beams above. Move to
the rear of the loft where there are no windows and wait a few
seconds for eyes to adjust.

Against the back wall are built-in bookshelves with racing
trophies—yellow-gold cars, crossed flags, silver-plated chalices,
a bronze steering wheel—spaced evenly. Tacked to the side
walls are laminated newspaper articles. There's one clipping,
in color, featuring a young man chugging from a trophy cup.
Because he is trying to smile and drink at the same time or
maybe because people are clapping him on the back, Cooper
is spilling milk all over his racing suit. The boy has got a head
of knotty russet hair and half-closed eyes. Needle has seen all
these articles before, headlines reading, *Welcome Home! Local
Man Rises from the Ashes to Race Again*, *Super Cooper Snatches
Victory out of the Jaws of Defeat*, and *Hometown Favorite Races
Like He's on a Mission*. The article headlined, *Tragic Crash Takes
the Life of Pit Survivor*, is missing from the wall. In that article
the journalist described how Cooper's neck *snapped gently*, a
detail Needle cannot forget.

When he turns toward the front of the barn Needle is startled by someone sitting in a rocking chair near the window.
His first instinct is to scurry down the ladder and he takes two
quick steps toward the loft door. Relax, though, it is no one
really, just the back of Cooper's sunburst-red helmet cradled
atop the chair's arm, his worn uniform draped along the back.
See the visor's down. Needle's face is stretched gaunt in the
mirrored reflection, a quick-nervous twitch pulsing under his
left eye.

Rest for a minute—just a minute—in the rocker. Enjoy how good the burn feels in the lower back when sitting. Let the heart return to beating like it should. Notice the groove in the floor where Minnie has been doing hard rocking. Test the rhythm of the chair. Pretend you are not yourself.

Now be distracted by the sudden flash of wings in the morning light, outside the window. Get up. Hang the hawk-flag; frighten the swallows.

# PIEBALD

When Lungs gives me the nod I lean into my snare and start an earnest drum roll. The bugle bleats out that melancholic Taps ditty the way Lungs has played it forever. On his mark, old Otis shoulders the rifle with a little difficulty and begins blasting his twenty-one gun salute. Mourners huddled around the hole flinch as the gunshot rattles off the headstones and away. They're blanks, nothing to fear.

I'm not counting, but after fifteen or sixteen shots the rifle stops and Otis says, "Sweet Jesus" as he crumples to the earth. Little American flags blow all around. Lungs pulls off the bugle and struggles to gather his breath. Those silently gathered regard Otis as if he were a pile of raked leafs on a windy day. The man in the hole is forgotten. I watch Lungs amble over to Otis to give mouth-to-mouth. Lungs, though, has emphysema, it's all he can do to bugle through Taps three or four times a day and that's with plenty of hits from the inhaler between numbers, so he won't be blowing much into Otis. A pair of gravediggers hustles to help, but Lungs brushes them off, cradles his pal, and lifts his head to wail at the sky. It is such a small noise. By the time I realize that I'm still rolling the snare and quit it, the cry is finished and we are left in that remaining relative silence that hangs on those befuddled watching a tragedy unfold.

There isn't much to dying, heart just stops, etc. Then to the ground. It's all ceremony and contemplation afterward. Since Lungs was a bugler in an old war, he knows lots of ancient, patriotic people soon to be deceased who are either not willing to travel or not invited to Arlington National Cemetery. So, he formed our troupe, *The Final Note*. We play Taps at funerals. Lungs found me kneeling beside my son's grave burying a letter in the dirt. I happened to be in the right place at the right time. He had seen me before. He asked how I paradiddled.

"Once, I had been a different man," I said.

He didn't know anyone who could keep it up for too long.

"I can't seem to put it down," I explained.

He found two thin sticks and handed them to me.

I stood and rattled those twigs on Buster Winslow's (1905-69) headstone until they snapped.

Now, on my drive home, I notice a dark splotch on the underside of my wrist. The car swerves. My skin has been discoloring for almost a year now. Until this new one the spots have only appeared on my chest and lower abdomen and I've been able to keep them concealed. My wife hasn't seen me shirtless since the accident at the lake. She sleeps in our son's room. The skin doctor told me there were more types of rashes than I could imagine and my condition was one of them. He gave me pills that made my mouth water and my elbows twitch. I tossed them. The psychologist told me that when we are speckled and rotten on the inside, we grow splotchy and grotesque on the outside. "Normally," he said, "this is metaphorical. But in your case…" He punched me in the shoulder and we shook our heads as if we couldn't believe it all. He told me not to worry and gave me a list of ten ways to inner peace. I've been up and down that list.

My wife, Savannah, and I met in a band in the Seventies. She played guitar. We rock and rolled. Soon, responsibilities. Her mother started to die and needed watching. The band broke up. Savannah and I married and moved in with mom. I found a job as a statistician. Savannah's mom died. We moped around for a while. Then Savannah started working for an accountant and we bought a house and a boat and lived. This bothered Savannah more than it did me. She wanted happiness without the hassle. I was willing to try. I told her I'd get another job, she could find another band. Instead, she got pregnant.

At home my wife is playing basketball in the drive so I park on the street. She's getting better. Physical activity is good. Soon, maybe we'll be able to communicate again. She needs help on her technique. The new orange ball bounces off the rim and rolls into the garage.

"Loosen your wrists," I say, carrying my snare and sticks toward the house.

Savannah has recently chopped her brown hair short. She doesn't wear skirts or dresses anymore. She bites her nails more than I'd like her to. Last month she had braces put on her straight-enough teeth. I understand the desire to look differently, sometimes I wear a hat to work, but she's made herself into somebody else.

"Thanks, Pop," she says.

I'm surprised that there's no sarcasm in her voice.

"What time is dinner?" she asks.

"Seven," I say.

"I'm going over to Miranda's for a while. Can I borrow the car?"

When our son Connor died, Savannah didn't speak for about two months. I became good at reading her mind. I'd find television channels she seemed to like, and cook small meals she'd stomach if I made them just right. Our shrink said to be patient. I didn't see any other choice. Eventually, she broke down and cried and cried for three weeks. Doctor said it was necessary to let the hurt go. I wanted to know where it was going and what would be left. She dried up, took long walks. Doc said that where the body meanders the head follows. Sometimes I'd go with her, but I couldn't keep up. She moved fast, went far, returned late. Once, I followed her on Connor's bike. She didn't flinch when she passed the cemetery and kept strolling to a children's playground on the other side of town. She sat on a bench and watched the kids with an unsettling smile. She convinced a small boy to let her push him on the swing. I reported this to the shrink. He's always quick to explain how perfectly natural it is for a mother to express herself in seemingly-unnatural ways, which I can appreciate, but he didn't see the distant look on her face when she was behind the kid. I decided to direct the walks to the cemetery. I figured we could grieve together at the headstone. When we arrived, I cried and waited for her to do the same. She bit at a piece of loose skin on her thumb and hummed softly. I asked what was wrong and she said she preferred walking alone. The psychologist suggested we get back to our roots. I was hoping we'd get back to the root we started together. Savannah picked the guitar back up. She went to Connor's old high school and posted a *Guitar Lessons* sign. A half dozen kids came. Then there was the incident on open-mike night at the coffee house. Now Savannah's only got Miranda, a sweet girl who really wants to master the fret board.

My wife is waiting for a reply.

"Of course," I say, tossing her the keys, "of course."

Inside, on the kitchen counter, I find a crossword puzzle Savannah's been working on. I don't think she's gotten a single

word right. There are places where she tried to use an eraser on
the ink. Outside, the tires on my car scream.


Before I go to our beaten shed at the cemetery the next morning, our office, I buy a florescent-yellow wristband from an
athletic shoe store to cover my discolored wrist.

The shed is near the road and we've had trouble with van-
dals and hooligans spray-painting our doors and stealing our
things. They take whatever they can. I saw a young man in
an ice cream joint wearing a company shirt that he'd stolen. I
confronted him with a lot of energy. Then we stood there both
knowing I was all talk. I told him he should be ashamed of
himself as he left. The bell above the door jingled.

When we aren't performing, Lungs is out promoting *The
Final Note* in neighboring graveyards and funeral homes. He
has red-white-and-blue flyers that do most of the selling. He
has written me a note: *Otis needs to be properly buried. He was
a patriot. You won't find a shooter of his caliber, but we need one
anyhow. Dead bodies don't wait for the living. I could tell you
stories about rank soldiers in WW II. I won't, I know you've got a
delicate stomach. Otis goes down tomorrow. Hire someone who can
fire a gun like a man. I'd hire a veteran myself, but I don't want
another friendship casualty on my watch. I posted an add in the
paper. Use the interview questions I've provided. That's all.*

Lungs will never let me live down an upset stomach I had
months ago from some bad pork. I was drum rolling along
and got sick. I was tactful about it and didn't miss more than
a couple beats. Lungs filed it away in his memory under my
folder of weaknesses and is quick to point it out.

While I'm waiting for coffee to brew in our most recent
coffee pot, I visit Connor's grave. The weather is fine; sky im-

placably blue, trees in good humor, headstones somber. The grass is getting long, someone should notify the groundskeeper. Connor's marker is made of black marble with isolated flecks of granite you don't notice unless you look hard. My wife and I didn't want anything fancy written or anything obviously religious overshadowing our boy. Just the stone, his name, and dates.

I crouch down and let a few moments pass.

Back at our shed, a bald man with a weak chin has poured himself a cup of coffee and is pacing. As I approach he shades his eyes with a big hand.

After a few questions, I know he's not right.

When the pot of coffee is empty, I make more. Five men, a boy, and a female firefighter apply. I ask them Lungs' questions and scrutinize their personalities. A man salutes me and I know he won't get the job. Someone whistles a tune I can't place. My interviewees get coffee breath, which makes sense, we're drinking coffee, and if they go without, they're dismissed, but I don't want to smell burnt beans from people's mouths. I have to shoo away a farmer who breathes his breakfast all over me.

When the man with one pale arm, one sunburned arm, sits down for the interview, I know I'm going to hire him before I begin the questions. He too has skin issues.

"What happened to your arm?" I ask.

"I used to drive a truck," he says.

"Ever fire a gun?"

The man, Snyder, has yellow hair and a thin handlebar moustache. He has a fat lip. Tiny flakes of dandruff shake down into his black coffee.

"Hell," Snyder says.

I retrieve a silk-screened *The Final Note* collared shirt while he sips his coffee like an Englishman.

After locking the shed, I saunter over to my son's grave. The cemetery is big enough for privacy when you want it. I lie in the grass and say mental things to my son. Then the chiggers get to me. I scratch my legs and notice a dark splotch above the ankle. I pull my socks up.

The groundskeeper's house is next to the lake on the other side of the graveyard. His hedges need clipping. I knock on the front door. When nobody answers I move around back. The metal gate door is open and the backyard slopes down to a wooden bench overlooking the lake. I sit and force myself to look at the water. It's not so bad. The sun is setting and the whippoorwills are calling out to one another.

I lost my son on the Fourth of July. I knew people would be coming out for the evening fireworks but I thought we'd have a few hours to kill before the lake became seriously congested. Connor wanted to water-ski. He was good at it. He only need-ed one ski. He argued about the life vest, but Savannah insist-ed. I inched the boat forward, pulling the rope tight as gently as I could, like preparing to yank out a loose baby tooth. Then I leaned on the throttle and he was up and gliding across the water. I remember Savannah shouting that he needed a haircut and I said, *Nah, nah, let it grow*. I don't think she heard me; it wasn't something I wanted to fight the wind for, just a state-ment that was half-thought, half-conversation. Connor had his jaw set as he crossed over the wake to the smoother water where he could see the shadow of himself with bent knees, straining arms outstretched like a sleepwalker, racing forward; behind us.

I've never met the groundskeeper but I've seen him. He's overweight and sweaty. I'm taller than he is. I haven't had any-thing to say to him before now, not that I could have, he is always with a loud machine. He probably knows the grass is getting long, that's his business. I rise from the bench and cross back over the lawn in the twilight. When I'm nearly to the gate, I hear a woman laugh. This startles me enough to freeze. She goes right on laughing. It's coming from the second-story window, I believe, but I can't see her through the tedious branches of a weeping willow. I call out. She finishes her laugh. I call again and the silence that follows seems to usher in night quicker than I think necessary. When I'm nearly at the gate, she bursts out laughing again. I hurry through the headstones to my car.

Lungs has decided to wear his Korean War uniform for Otis's burial. I have on khaki slacks to cover the dark spots I found on my knees and calves this morning. It's hot today with no breeze. I use my yellow wristband to dab at my forehead as we wait for our shooter, Snyder. I told him high-noon and it's a quarter after now. Lungs has been scowling at me for the last half-hour. There are about twenty people melting in their black funeral outfits. The minister had to take off. Otis is in the hole and we've eulogized long enough. I read a poem about autumn written by an obscure poet.

Otis isn't our only job today. We've got a retired colonel and a carpenter who was in the navy for a summer in the 1940's at a ritzy cemetery on Meadowview. Families have given us a deposit.

When Snyder finally shows up he is dressed in shorts and a tank-top. His sunburned arm stands out from the rest of his pale skin like it's something separate from his body. His swollen lip has healed. Lungs reluctantly hands over the rifle and pants. When Lungs gets angry, it's harder for him to breathe.

"Let's remember Otis, now," I say. "And do this one right for him."

Snyder appears as if he's been out prowling all night. His shoes have speckles of yellow and red paint on them. By way of an apology, he shrugs. Lungs tries to calm himself by smoothing out his uniform. I wet my lips and begin the drum roll.

The day passes difficultly. Snyder doesn't put his heart into the job and his timing is off. The rifle is supposed to be angled at about seventy-five degrees and he holds it around sixty. The last shot should be fired when Lungs plays the final note on the bugle. Snyder finished about half-way through the ditty, set the rifle to the ground to lean on, and picked his teeth. For the dead carpenter, he only fired nineteen shots and the family demanded a refund. Lungs was fuming. He tried to lecture Snyder, but the old man takes so long to get words out, Snyder cut him off with a flourish of his hands. Later, I asked Lungs if I should terminate the new shooter. After consideration, Lungs said, "No...he's in...my army. I'll...break him...good."

At home Miranda is playing an acoustic guitar and Savannah is singing, in the living room. When I come in, they stop. I set my car keys in a porcelain bowl by a plant.

"Hello," Miranda says. She has small, oval glasses, hair in a long braid, and petite ears. My wife is wearing a baseball cap crookedly, earringless as usual. She is on the sofa with her legs crossed ankle atop knee.

"Hi, Miranda, hello Savannah," I say.

Savannah's foot shakes.

"You ladies need a drummer?"

Miranda glances nervously at my wife who is unsmiling. She might be in a black mood.

"How about you find someplace else to be?"

I have nowhere to go. I stand blinking for a few moments. Miranda is trying to hide behind her guitar and Savannah has narrowed her pale eyes. I put my hand in the bowl for my car keys.

The groundskeeper doesn't answer when I knock on the front door again. Neither does the laughing woman. In the backyard, at the bench, the lake looks peaceful. I see a sailboat ablaze with the remaining sun on the horizon. My old speedboat has been in the water since the accident. I haven't gotten around to selling it and the marina owner isn't charging me for the slip space, so it sits.

I remember thinking that my boy would be OK because he was bobbing in the water, buoyed by the life vest. There was still motion and possibility. The first person out to him, a man who had been in the other boat, recoiled in that instant of contact and the horror on his face, as he tread water, reluctant to touch Connor, broke my wife into a kind of hysterics that drowned my ability to comprehend. My instinct was to console Savannah, shelter her grief, tell her *It will be fine.*

I'm pretty sure the laughing woman in the window has been watching me since I sat down on the bench. It feels like there are eyes on me. I can't see her, though, with the willow in the way. I approach the house cautiously, measuring my footsteps in the grass. Though I was expecting it, when I see her silhouette framed in the window, I'm surprised.

"Hello?" I say.

She doesn't respond. I can't seem to communicate with women lately.

She has slight shoulders and long hair. It's too dark for features. When I take a few steps toward the gate she starts to laugh. I stop. It is a mature laugh, experienced. A young girl isn't wise enough to laugh like this and an old woman wouldn't have the constitution to laugh this loudly.

"What's funny?" I ask.

Her laughter echoes away.

"Maybe you could tell me the joke?"

She doesn't respond. Perhaps she is mentally challenged. But no, the laugh is too warm to be insane. This could just be coy.

"I don't mean to impose," I say, taking a step forward and gesturing with my hands. "I wanted to remind the ground-skeeper…" She cuts me off with her laughter. I lean against the willow tree. Her hair flutters. It's like a tree fort under the canopy of branches.

"Well, that's not the only reason I'm here, you're right to laugh at me. There's the view. I haven't looked at the lake in a long time."

She becomes silent, listening.

"I lost my son there, you see. Perhaps you read about it in the papers?"

When she doesn't reply, I am grateful. I shouldn't be so quick to talk about Connor. Since when do I use my dead son as a topic of conversation with a woman I'm mildly flirting with in the window?

She seems to be thinking.

"Well, anyway. I'm sorry to bother you. Could you tell the groundskeeper I stopped by? I work here, by the way. Well, I mean, I'm a drummer for *The Final Note*. We play Taps at funerals. You probably heard us and didn't know it. If you have any questions about the lawn or want to talk you or he could stop by the office on the other side of the cemetery…" She laughs at this. "Right. You're right, it's just a shed. I'm leaving now, thanks for listening."

I shut the gate behind me and pass through the darkening cemetery, dejected. I've got to learn to be more confident when I talk to ladies. Straight forward.

A band of hooligans with plastic masks approach me. I'm in no mood to run and am prepared for their minor beating. One of the men holds them back, for some reason.

"Where have you been?" he asks.

I'm pretty sure the voice is Snyder's. I figured he was too old for this.

"Looking at the lake."

"The groundskeeper's house?"

"Sure."

"Did you hear the crazy woman?" a smaller hooligan asks.

"I spoke to a lady in the window, but she isn't mad."

The masked Snyder decides to run forward, give me a wedgie, and shove me to the ground. The others hoot and run into the darkness.

I order pizza for dinner because I'm not in the mood to cook. We eat from paper plates in front of the television. Savannah has the controller. I ask her what she thinks of adoption.

Her braces are filled with crust and sauce.

I repeat myself.

She tries to turn the volume on the television up.

"You were a wonderful mother."

She squirms on the couch. "I don't want to talk about this," she says.

It's hard to miss a splotchy discoloration that has appeared on my forearm. I slap my hand over it. I tell myself, *Straight forward.*

"We need to talk now."

"I can't cope with you," she says, getting up from the couch and climbing to the second floor. Connor's bedroom door slams.

On the television, some teenage drama unfolds.


When I get to the cemetery late, Snyder is already there, thankfully. Lungs asks if the world is coming to an end or what? He wants to know if time has changed and he hasn't been notified. By the look in his eyes, I can tell he wants to smack me. Also, he questions if we had ever heard of proper attire. Snyder is in his *The Final Note* shirt but has cut the short sleeves off. His pale arm is having difficulty turning as red as his other arm. I'm wearing pants and a green, long-sleeved shirt. This morning I noticed a dark dot behind my ear so I combed my hair over it. I saw the skin doctor before work and he asked if I had been taking the pills. I said, "Yes, and they're not working." He produced a scalpel and took a graft of my patchy skin. I wanted to know what was happening to me.

"Do they itch?" he asked.

"No," I said.

"If they start to, don't scratch them."

"How many cases have you seen like this?"

The doctor had my medical folder open and he muttered something into it and left the tiny, clinical room. I waited and looked at the framed pictures of gonorrhea, herpes, toe fungus, and mumps on the walls. When he returned he had pills he insisted were stronger and told me that on the plus side, it didn't look like cancer yet, on the minus side, he couldn't find any examples of people like me. He made me undress and took some Polaroid's while sucking on his teeth and clucking his tongue.

Now, I'm on the pills, and my elbows are jittering like crazy. I drum roll faster than Taps requires. Snyder holds the rifle at the appropriate degree and fires on time. However, when he gets to the last shot, he lowers the gun and blasts it at Lungs. It's just powder, but the implications are grave. Lungs botches the final note. I hurry to get a drink of water when we are done while Lungs begins a short-winded tirade. Snyder chuckles and kicks a bit of dirt on Lungs' shoes.

Our next few funerals are tense. When Rear Admiral Peepler goes down Snyder blows a bubble of gum that pops all over his bristly face. Afterwards, the rifle gets sticky and Lungs tries to chew Snyder out. Snyder says he'll clean it at home. Lungs won't let the weapon out of his sight. There are senti-mental reasons. At the end of the day, Snyder refuses to hand it over. After a brief and awkward struggle with the gun, Snyder shouts something incoherent and shoves Lungs to the ground. The old man gasps and makes a terrible, throaty noise. I help him with the breathalyzer.

"Do you want me to fire him?"

Lungs can't speak, but he shakes his head.

"He shouldn't push you around."

Lungs wants to deliver a speech.

"I think he may be in cahoots with the hooligans around here."

"Proof?" Lungs manages.

"I don't have anything hard."

"Get it."

Lungs struggles to stand. There is a dead leaf in his hair that he doesn't let me pick out. He rubs his hands together and his dry lips tremble with excitement. This is him scheming.

Snyder is next to a sarcophagus close to our shed. His back is to me. When I approach, he swings the rifle around and stops it just short of my skull.

"Kee-Cha!" he says.

I back off.

"Wood and muscle to head equals cottage cheese for you!"

My elbows twitch.

"Ha," I say. "That would have hurt."

He twirls the rifle over his head and begins to pantomime beating me with it. I try to stand still.

"I'm going to put a bayonet on this so I can carve!"

"Snyder," I say, "maybe you should find another line of work?"

He slings the rifle over his shoulder and leans against the stone grave. "I don't think so," he says. "I'm getting paid to shoot a gun. My friends can't believe it. They want to know if we need more shooters. If we hire five or six of my pals we can take turns getting to twenty-one. All stand around the hole, bang, bang, bang, from the sides."

I slide my hands in my pockets and glance at the clouds.

"Looks like your sweetie was smooching on you good," Snyder says, touching the rifle tip to my neck.

He's mistaking a splotch for passion. I back away and pull my collar high over my neck.

On my way to the groundkeeper's house, I snag a lily from a bouquet at Speed Turlington's (1927-1994) grave. I try to sneak up to the window, but she laughs when I'm near enough to see her silhouette. She must have been expecting me.

"Hi again," I whisper loudly, keeping the flower behind my back.

I swallow hard and wait for her to quiet down.

"You spend a lot of time at that window. The view must be exquisite."

She doesn't respond. Perhaps she thinks I'm expecting to be invited into her bedroom, which I'm not, of course.

I raise the lily toward the window. She begins that familiar laughter. There is kindness in it.

"I admire your humor," I say. "I hope you don't think of this as a come on. I just happened to see it and I thought of you. It doesn't mean anything, much, I mean. It's not a rose."

She stops laughing.

"I'm going to leave it here by the tree. Feel free to come down when you're comfortable. I've got work to do now. Take care."

I set the lily on the ground and walk lightly to the office.

The reference phone number Snyder used on his job application connects me to a self-help hotline. I'm supposed to press the appropriate number on the phone pad: 1 for suicidal tendencies, 2 for unrelenting depression, 3 for excessive happiness, 4 for euphoric highs followed by excruciating lows, 5 for coping with loss, 6 for…I press 5 and am told it will cost me a dollar a minute. I'm fine with this. A recorded woman comes on the line and slowly starts to describe a gentle brook in a dale with a deer loping beneath the sun. Now I'm supposed to picture myself, a myself unmarred by the hurt, honey-dipped and happy, fit to be skipping along in the dale with the deer under the sun. I'm golden and carefree. Here is my boy by my side. We're together, by the brook. It's nice. Connor is reminding me how to skip. The woman on the phone tells me I can be happy. Connor and I skip to the top of a hill and then he flies away. I imagine the woman in the window with the voice of the woman on the phone, directing me to happiness.

On my way back to see if she has retrieved the lily, I stop at Connor's grave. I pick at the high grass above him. Over near an eight foot obelisk, I see Lungs with a group of old-timers huddled together. When I wave, Lungs turns his back to me. I creep close enough, darting behind headstones and lingering behind a dying oak, to hear them whispering conspiratorially.

"What about the cops?" a man with cataracts asks.

"I'll…pay…them…off," Lungs replies.

"How far do you want us to go?" someone wants to know.

"Gentlemen…" Lungs says, "this…is hallowed…ground. We…go…all the way."

A squirrel drops a nut from the tree I'm hiding behind. The old men clam up and wait for further noises. There are always noises in cemeteries, particularly after dusk, and it doesn't take long for them to be distracted by something else away from me. They shuffle off. The air the old men leave behind holds a heaviness that makes me tired.

At home, Savannah is weeping in our son's bedroom. She has forgotten to lock the door so I let myself in and drop down on his bed. When I place my arm around her she vehemently tosses it aside. No matter. I curl myself up and wait for Savannah to stop shouting and hitting me in the back of the head. I wish the comforter still smelled like Connor because I've forgotten his scent. The sheets smell like my wife which is good in its own way.

Even though I've been on the pills, splotches keep appearing. There's one on my cheek, and I noticed a dark patch on my tongue when I brushed my teeth this morning. I decided not to shower because I didn't have the courage to see how speckled I've become. *The Final Note* shirt is on over my turtleneck. I slept in my son's room last night and Savannah spent the night at Miranda's. My wife has moved into a different kind of grief. I think she's trying to actually *be* our son. In Connor's shirt drawer I found a dark-colored diary she has been keeping from his point of view. There are a lot of complaints about me, whom she refers to as Dad, written on the pages. The most recent entry admitted to having sexual feelings for Miranda.

I drop by the shrink's office for direction. He tells me I need to talk to her and then changes the subject to my patchy face.

I head to the cemetery and brew some coffee. Lungs arrives with a friend who drives a hearse.

"What...news?"

"There's a good chance our shooter's not on the up and up."
Lungs' breath smells like formaldehyde.

"He wanted to know if we would hire his friends to help
with the salute."

"Good. Hire...them. We've only...got one...perfor-
mance...today. Sgt. Haver...man...at five. Be...prepared,"
Lungs says, pinching my arm.

I finish the pot of coffee and drive to the doctor's office.
He takes me off the pills and snaps more Polaroid's. I ask him
how I should explain this to my wife. He's surprised she doesn't
know already. I try to change the subject but he is a man un-
daunted. Finally, I muster enough guts to tell him it's none of
his business and I try to storm out to the car emphatically.

Back at the cemetery Snyder and five of his friends have
managed to pull the shed up from whatever was holding it
down and are rocking it back and forth. I'm hoping they'll scat-
ter when they see me, but they don't. Snyder has taped a steak
knife to the rifle.

"What happened to your face?" he asks.

His friends gather around me with their spray-cans and
baseball bats.

"I've been getting these dark splotches all over my body."
Somebody asks if I'm contagious.

"I think they have something to do with my dead son."

"I didn't know you lost a son, man," Snyder says. His friends
grimace in sympathy. We all have a moment of silence. I notice
the grass has been cut. The groundskeeper finally did his job.

I tell them they're all hired. They look suspicious for a moment but then give each other high fives. Someone cheers and
spray paints the air. Maybe these guys are misunderstood.

At Connor's grave, the grass is soft and bugless. We have a one-sided mental conversation. I tell him about the woman in the window. I want him to know that I still love his mother. A rainbow sprinkler cascades over the plot of Bennet family.

The groundskeeper has trimmed the hedges and clipped the willow in his backyard. The lily is gone. At the bench I shade my eyes with a speckled hand and gaze at the water. If I believed in the soul and the soul had shape and color it'd look like the lake. Blue-black and shimmering, I imagine.

When I am nearly to the willow, the woman laughs. I've come to tell her it's over. In this much daylight, she is easy to see. Her mouth is open and round, eyes staring and faded; everything made of plastic.

A window in another room slides open and the groundskeeper glares down the barrel of a shotgun at me. A trickle of sweat slips down his red forehead.

"She's a mannequin?" I ask.

"You're trespassing," the groundskeeper replies. He has an accent I can't place.

"But she laughs."

"I'm either shooting or calling the cops. Which is it?"

"I came by a few days ago to tell you that the grass needed cutting. I wanted to thank you for taking care of it now."

"There's a front door."

"From your bench, the lake."

The groundskeeper relaxes.

"It's been helpful to spend some time back here," I say.

I don't know why, but something in me goes out. I try to choke down the emotion rising from my gut. "That woman had me fooled," I blurt, shaking my head.

"You're supposed to be frightened. I've got her hooked up to a continuous laugh track and a motion detector. If a prowler gets too close to the house, they set her off."

"Isn't that something?"

"Were you trying to talk to her?"

"No."

"You looked like you were ready to speak there for a moment. What were you going to say?"

"Nothing."

"I found a flower."

I scratch my chin.

He lifts the gun again. "You some kind of sickie, sir?"

"Let me go," I plead.


Savannah is not home when I arrive. My face, reflected from a hanging frying pan in the kitchen, looks like a diseased leaf. I rummage through the winter clothes in the basement. When I put on Connor's red ski mask I breathe in a hint of his scent through the odor of mothballs. I remember snowmen, ice skates, plastic sleds, runny noses, and the little clouds of our breath blooming and disappearing.

I get stuck in traffic on my way back to the cemetery. Drivers stare at me in my mask. I try to keep my eyes forward.

The cemetery is mostly quiet when I arrive. I take my snare and drumsticks to the burial ground. There are about a dozen old men dressed in fatigues around the hole. I recognize them as members of a radical VFW. Every year they have a parade. Lungs has borrowed a Vietnam Tiger Stripe camouflage uniform for the occasion and there is a battered pistol at his side. One of the mourners sees me, says, "Incoming!" loudly enough for everyone to hear, awkwardly drops to a knee, and pulls a rusted knife from his combat boot. The other men clumsily produce weapons and glare at me.

I pause and raise my drumsticks.

Lungs says, "Is that...you?"

I say, "Yes."

"It's OK..." Lungs tells the men, "he's...one of...ours."

The men hide their weapons and try to look like they're grieving.

"Get...over...here."

I approach cautiously.

"Your disguise...may fool...them. Good...idea...comrade."

As Lungs hits his inhaler, Snyder and his friends approach. The old man's wet eyes widen. The hooligans are wearing *The Final Note* shirts tucked into clean pants with clean-shaven faces and combed hair. Snyder proudly marches ahead with the rifle.

"I'm glad you've changed your tune, old man," Snyder says to Lungs. "Your friends will enjoy seeing us young soldiers honoring the men who fought to let us stand here today. Men like you, Lungs."

Lungs fidgets as he tries to gauge the sincerity of Snyder's speech.

"I'll pass the rifle around if that's alright with you," Snyder says.

"Suit...yourself...soldier."

The minister mutters something about bravery and places his hand on a Bible. I can see the steel-toed boots peeking out from beneath his robes.

Lungs gives me the nod and I fall into a comfortable drum roll. Snyder shoulders the rifle; the steak knife catches a bit of sunlight and blinds me for an instant. I hear the bugle. Then a small old man pops out of the coffin and tosses a tear bomb at Snyder and his friends. They are surprised by this. Perhaps they were ready to turn over a new leaf. The man in the coffin scrambles out of the hole and scurries behind the others who have brandished their weapons and are scowling.

I quit rattling the drum and get out of the way. Snyder curses and swats at his eyes. There is a moment when I think they'll retreat, but Snyder lowers his makeshift bayonet and charges. The hooligans advance.


Miranda refuses to open the door when I knock. She can see me through the peephole and won't let me explain the ski mask. She threatens to unleash a mean dog in the backyard I've never seen.

Savannah is at the playground. The sun is low in the monkey bars. She is sitting on a swing but not swinging. I drop on the empty plastic seat next to her and the metal above groans.

"Why are you wearing his mask?"

That's hard to explain. I should just take it off.

"Miranda's Mom fired me this afternoon."

I try to lean over on my swing and console Savannah, but the chain won't let me reach.

"Really, there's more to it than that. You probably haven't noticed that I've been trying my best to think and act how Connor might have. I've been watching MTV, lifting weights, and rebelling against you."

"I read the diary," I say quietly.

"God," she says, standing. "Why did you pry into my personal things?"

Her empty swing quivers.

I rise and try to put my hand across her back.

"Don't touch me. Just leave me alone. I can't stand you always hovering. You make me feel so down. Is this the kind of father you would have been? You're terrible. Connor would have hated you snooping into his things."

"I'm sorry, Savannah. I take what I can get. I don't want you to be him. He's gone. You've been gone, too. I want you back. We can get through this together."

She spins and hurries away from me. This talk is no use. Our psychologist is full of shit.

I follow Savannah in my car as she speed-walks along the shoulder of the road. I pray that she doesn't scamper off into the woods where I will lose her. I put on my emergency blinkers. Other cars pass and frown at me, masked and following a woman on a dusky road. They don't know anything. After a mile, Savannah stops and waits for me to drive up next to her.

"You're not going away, are you?"

I try to respond gently with my eyes.

She gets in the car, reaches for my mask. The automatic seatbelt holds her.

"Not yet."

As we pass, the cemetery is aglow with police lights. Things there have gotten out of hand. I'll check on Connor's headstone first thing in the morning.

The marina is nearly vacant. Night is excusing day with a ridged moon. Savannah waits in the car as I try to start our speedboat. I have to coax it alive. While the engine catches itself, I wait for my wife to decide what she's going to do. I have the car keys. She could walk home but in the back of her mind she knows I'll follow her again.

Eventually she steps out of the car and down to the dock.

"What are you doing?" she asks.

"We haven't been on the water."

"There's a reason for that."

"Let's not be afraid."

Water laps against the side of the boat.

Once she is on board, I circle the perimeter of the lake in order to remember how to move across water. Then I find the center, where we had been before, and cut the engine. I toss the ski-line behind us. We drift along.

"What are you doing?" Savannah asks. She has been quiet up until now. Her face, in the wind, with the hair away, looks remarkably like I remember Connor's; defiant and smooth.

I turn my back on her and take off the mask, my shirt, and my pants. The moon points out the splotches decorating my skin. Behind me Savannah gasps. I imagine, maybe, she is reaching out to touch me instead of recoiling in disgust.

Closing my eyes, I cast the ski overboard and hurl myself in after it.

# SAILOR MAN

The phone rings and wakes the baby up and it's after midnight and for a moment there before the clamor it was quiet and nice. Answering the phone this late is never a good idea. Last time I picked up the receiver after midnight I heard word from a groggy nurse that my mother had passed, which was a surprise since everyone knew it was my father's time to go.

Tracy rises from the bed and ignores my plea to not-answer it—probably just a wrong number—and says "Hello?" and while she's listening wordlessly to the person on the other line and the baby somehow, miraculously, drifts back to sleep, it occurs to me that I don't know anyone anymore I care about who could be calling with bad news and this makes me feel momentarily invincible.

"That was your uncle," Tracy says, hanging up the phone. Her voice is alert and sharp; ever-ready. This is the New Her, super-thankful to God that we, already in our forties, were able to change our minds and decide to have a child after all, and did.

"Oh."

"He's spooked. There's a noise upstairs."

"Big old house."

"Would you be a doll and check on him?"

"In the morning."

"He can't sleep."

"Yeah, well."

"He lost his only brother, you know."

I know I don't have a choice here and she's right, of course, he's all that's left of my family other than the family I've created and I know that if I keep protesting Tracy will threaten to simply go herself and will, it is not a bluff. I rise and dress and make my way to the door with my keys and say, "I'll be back soon."

"Honey," she calls, "don't forget to grab my keys."

This is something I had forgotten: my pickup's in the shop with a busted radiator, her keys are in her purse in the closet. "Got them," I reply, too loudly, I hear our son stir and before I can hear if he is going to fuss or not I am outside and in my wife's Subaru and negotiating the frozen roads. It is not dark with the low, gray clouds and a number of cars out and about, it is Saturday night and I am among these people with late-night plans.

I pull right up to the front steps of my childhood home, do not go around back to the detached garage, stop the car, enter into the foyer where my uncle Drake is standing, fretting, offering a greeting I don't pay any attention to and when I am in I take off my shoes like I've done since I was a boy. It is hot inside, my uncle's got the furnace working overtime, and I'm automatically thinking about heating bills and what this must cost and how it gets paid.

Drake's the spitting image of my father minus thirty-or-so pounds of muscle. There's the fringe of whimsical hair over the big ears, the small-crooked nose, weak, double-chin, gray mustache, heavy-set English eyes with super-long lashes. The old man is going on and on, "…been calling, you know," and I cut him off and tell him never to call my house again.

"There's a noise, upstairs."

I steal a quick look over at my uncle and am surprised to see a glimmer of terror there.

"Probably a mouse."

"It ain't a dang rodent. And if it were I can't get up there to kill it!" he says, loud and sputtering. The old man is so easily worked-up, the noise must be driving him mad, he's probably been staggering around from room to room imagining what the sound could possibly be, if the noise even exists in the first place, and in this empty house maybe Drake's losing his mind a little.

"Maybe it's a ghost," I say quietly, spookily, wiggling my fingers in front of his face.

"I told you it wasn't a mouse!" the old man shouts.

"I said ghost, Drake. Ghost. Like the apparition of my mother trying to teach you a lesson. Maybe she's confused and thinks you're dad."

"Thinks I'm dead?" The old man's hands flap. He's got the ancient, elderly head-wobble.

I turn away, muttering for him to wait here even though this isn't necessary. Then I climb the groaning stairs.

When my mother's dementia worsened my father was quick to put a mattress in his trophy room so he could sleep at night. And at night is when mom needed him most. I know. I slept over—Tracy's suggestion—slouched in a recliner in their bedroom with an eye on my tiny mother swallowed up by the king-sized bed. She woke up awfully, confused and clawing for someone who wasn't there. I'd sit on the edge next to her and do what I could, *There, there, there, Mom, it's OK*, until the nightmare of her waking condition blew by.

Meanwhile, dad dreamed down the hall.

And this whole sleeping-in-separate rooms concept was my father's, no doubt about it, although the doctor believed it was a good idea since my father's heart was on its last legs, staggering and ready to drop—*one, two, three*—and the body needed rest now more than ever. Dad was the one dying. Doc said soon, *Any day*, the strain was real and too much. Tracy, who had a rocky relationship with her own crummy father, bought all this, believed she could see something absent in his eyes, thought we should do everything we could to ease the suffering, thought it'd be wise for him to spend time in the trophy room surrounded by everything he'd fought for. Tracy decided that someone should prepare mom for the inevitable so she could brace herself somehow, delicate as her mind was, she had a right to know. That burden fell upon my shoulders—I waited in her room for a pocket of lucidity, practicing my line—*Mom, Samuel's dying and you're going to have to let him go*—and my opportunity came around two in the morning after she had terribly awoken and danced through her horrible pantomime and I had soothed her like a champ and seen fair skies in her eyes—I told her what Tracy thought she had a right to hear. Mom, caught momentarily in reality with me, whispered, *You mean he's dead?* with her eyebrows furrowed and lips barely parted and with just enough energy to turn breath into words. Instead of trying to explain, *Well, not yet, technically...*I said, *Yes*, with confidence. Then she turned her head away, thoughtful, and we sat there for some time both mourning the man. Soon she let out a sob that shook her whole body, rolled onto her side, and eventually slipped into a fitful sleep. And if she remembered anything about it in the morning, I didn't know. And if she grew confused when she did see him from time to time when he'd sit with her in the late afternoons spooning potato soup, thought, *Hold on a second...* I never knew. None of this mattered. It was all a lie. I wish I'd never said a thing. Her heart relinquished first.

Through the raised mini-blinds I see flakes of snow drifting past the streetlight.

Down the hall is my dad's room. It has always been a place forbidden to enter. It smells sour. In glass cases are the spoils of a lifetime of amateur boxing—trophies, laminated newspaper snapshots, medallions, golden gloves, and plenty of belts. There are also piles of video tapes and journals filled with notes; he was as much a student of the sport as he was a competitor, he'd study his opponents' moves weeks prior to a match. Before I was born, when he was making a name for himself, so the story goes, my father started losing his hair early and he looked older than he was. His trainer, a man named Whip, put my father on a strict diet of lean meat, eggs, and vegetables. He stressed curls with great weight. Soon, dad had enormous arms—*The right one's made of iron, the left one's made of steel, if the right one doesn't git ya, than the left one will*—and looked, I suppose, a little like Popeye. Plus all those greens. Whip started calling dad the *Sailor Man* and my father, the boxer, was born. He got tattoos. He smoked a corncob pipe. He crushed tin cans of spinach with one hand. He squinted his right eye. In his hay-day they'd play the *Popeye* theme song as my father jogged down the aisle, shaking his arms loose, and into the ring. Growing up, whenever my father did a Popeye imitation—that skittering chuckle and garbled New England accent—I knew he was in a good mood and so mom and I were happy. But when he'd lose a match and come home bruised and rubbery the house held its breath as his anger simmered and boiled over with some reservoir of strength—energy enough to rattle the windows—he still had in him.

In his office now, I am surprised how little dust has settled on the place. His single bed by the window is unmade, something he would never stand for in life. The walls are festooned with framed championship certificates and titles. Tucked into an open closet is a leather medicine ball. There's a television tray with a clean plate and an unopened bottle of water on it. His desk is pushed against the back-wall and on it are a lamp and a framed picture of the Sailor Man in his youth with his arms thrown high, shirtless, and smiling wide with the mouthpiece out of a black-and-blue face. My mom snapped the shot. This was when they were young, before I was born, when she still attended his matches. When I came along, she quit going and never let me see him fight. Dad protested. Mom said if the *Sailor Man* wanted to sacrifice his body and get his brains bashed in, that was his choice, but the ring was no place for a boy. Dad didn't argue this; it probably didn't seem worth the effort. But I knew that he'd grown up around boxing and believed somehow being in the ring hardened him into a man. Me, I was forever Swee' Pea, the Softie. He loved me all right so long as he lived but never really thought much of me.

I hear a beep coming from my father's desk; the answering machine is flashing with twenty messages. I don't think it can handle more. This is the sound that's been haunting Drake.

The messages are complaints by people who have lost money in my father's vending machine. To be honest, I completely forgot about the thing. Maybe three or four years ago he purchased the machine. It gave him a reason to get out of the house and maybe make a few extra dollars. He put it outside the bus terminal, a location where people were always coming and going—I bet it was a wonderful place for him to meet women. He'd sit on a bench behind a newspaper and offer pretty ladies a free Coke and a bag of Fritos. Maybe he hopped on the bus with them from time to time—disappeared for the day.

I guess the Sailor Man posted this phone number, his private line—I don't know how the phone bills are being paid—on the machine. Seems as if customers haven't figured out that it is empty and that the owner is dead and gone and that it will never spit out a can of soda or a bag of chips again. I don't know who technically owns the thing and is responsible to refill it. I know it wasn't left to me.

One disgruntled guy has left maybe ten messages—the electronic voice on the machine mentions that the date of the final call came two days ago. The man may have continued calling if the answering machine was willing to keep listening. He speaks as if he has been personally offended—maybe he's a bus driver or a custodian who incredulously keeps hoping to get at something that's not there. On the machine, he's outraged and curses like it's practiced. He threatens to bash the vending machine with a baseball bat and calls my father a *fucking shyster*. In another message, the man says he's going to *hunt* my father down and get his money back *one way or another*.

I tug at the line in the wall and disconnect the phone.


Snow is falling and it fell all night and it is making me dizzy driving this morning. I pull over, stop the car, get out and look around. I'm in a snow-banked parking lot by the soccer field. The goals are ice-laced gateways. I shove my hands into my pockets. In the cold my wedding ring is loose on my finger hardly hampered by the knuckle. I make a fist around the change I've got, walk from the car down the slope, prints lingering in the snow, my breath wavers over me idiotically—

dumb-cloud, buffoon-thought, numb-brain—the head holds cold ears and watery eyes and enough doubt to sink me; now I'm on the creek and the ice and the feet splay.

The trees trick me into believing I'm swaying, not the snow-weary branches bending, not the glazed-over evergreen thistles, not the blackbirds barking at the air they stir, not gravity toying with the flakes falling, sky imploding. Nothing like that makes my knees chatter, lips twitch, tongue swell, nose pucker, mind, one-two-three, one-two-three-waltz along the creek-bed, nearly remembering enough now to properly cloud over what's been really bothering me—the Sailor Man—my footprints track back to the wife's car with the bells and the whistles, car still running, not near paid-for, but hell, a second car is *necessary* with my pickup in the shop, costing us time and money, and I know this whole car debacle is easily remedied once I just let go and fetch what's mine. I can see the Subaru over the rise— the exhaust is making weather of its own there in the wake of itself—tire tracks fading in the too-deep-to-drive-through snow—there's always the possibility that once I've driven in I cannot drive out; no matter, I can shove at the immovable all day, it's a thing I'm good at, leaning in and pushing with everything I've got.

What happens to the fishes under the ice, and the crawdads and the water-critters down below—some kind of cryogenics, a stasis, a reprieve, life-pause—waiting for the thaw?

Here's what I should do and here's when I should do it— here is not my destination but it's where I am—spar with the loss: Dad's dead and the anger I pent up during the years leading up to his departure has not died. Now, then; let it go. Breathe differently. Un-fog the head, un-clog the heart. So what about what was? Think more of the what-will-be and the who-to-become. If not for me, for Sam. Sammy. Not-Samuel—well, yes; Samuel—the name's part of it—*upper-cut, left, left, hook.* My boy back in the car.

I return in the spaces I made coming down the hill. The Subaru waits patiently, like a pet, a dog; my old dog Newt, rather, not-mine, which is the point—I was walking the thing in the early fall back before the Sailor Man had keeled over—a black Labrador, Newt, it trotting me along with the leash down the sidewalk on our way to the park or the playground or the thin leaf-speckled forest—us going toward wherever, happily; our specific memories bounding around in our heads like the time we played Frisbee, the time we chased squirrels, the time we splashed in the shallows, the time we caught colds, the time we curled upon the couch and watched Sports, the time Newt discovered fire, the time, the time—when, there, across the street from Newt and I, we spied a man walking his dog, a black Labrador, in the opposite direction and the man and dog turned to regard Newt and I regarding them and what a pair of idiots—a quadruple-bunch, as it were—morons, the lot of us, this man with half-smile and half-wave, his dog with half-smile and half-wave and Newt and I caught half-waving too—all of this preposterous, really, because the dog that the man on the other side of the road trotted behind looked exactly like Newt, there could be no meaningful difference, a black Lab that looked like the idea of a black Lab, if there were a line-up I'd never be able to tell the difference—*Here, Newt, boy; here*—and what a farce, this dog-thing, this pet-owning—that man and me, were we the same?

Now Newt's gone.

Sam is asleep in the car. I see him through the back window. His seat faces backwards so he can sort-of peer through the defrosting. There's nothing to see but gray-white in the sky and me peeking in, hands cupped to the glass, nose-cold—the father outside. Sammy is nestled in some kind of super-thick blue-colored body-suit so that only his face is exposed. I am so glad he looks like Tracy and not me. Her chin, nose, hairline, ears, mouth; all that—only thing he's got of mine are his eyes and I'm told their color may change. His cheeks are flushed, like he's blushing, although he cannot be; I've not yet taught him shame. He is five months and a handful-of-days old. He can hold his head up. He can say, *Ba-Ba-Ba* and *Um-ma-ma*. When he lets me, I stand over his crib and repeat—*Da-da*— so maybe he knows it's me—Da-da—the word, the name; the father who is learning to love in a way once removed from how he's loved before, a love I'm still figuring out, baby-steps, the Unconditional, an emotion I don't trust myself to feel yet, everything I've ever known has had conditions—the snow is really coming down now—my boy, my Lima Bean, Cherub, Bubaloo, Monkey, Peanuthead, still wearing pet names, I like any of them other than the one he was born with, Samuel, after my father, who died a week or ten days before Pumpkinface was born—if he had just died sooner or later Gremlin would have been named otherwise, something not-Him, but no, because of the proximity, Tracy suggested it to me, whispered in her wavering, serious, just-out-of-the-delivery-room and I-knew-it-was-going-to-be-a-boy voice—*Simon, let's name him Samuel*—and my answer—*No! No!*—issued forth in a wow-how-about-the-miracle-of-life-moment, kind-of non-voice; she didn't hear. Now I'm sandwiched between Samuel's and Buttercup's in the car warm and safe and I'm just going to go ahead and promise him and me right now, I'll just come out with it—*Son, I'm going to be the best father in the universe. No better, no how. I'm going to be nothing like your grandfather. Nope. A name's just a name, Newt knew that. You and I will get beyond what we're called. We'll get beyond what a thing means and focus on what just is: My soon-to-be unconditional—once I've got a bead on it—love for you and maybe down the line vice versa.*

Saying all this isn't half-bad for a moment and I think that maybe the reason I pulled over in the first place, to clear my mind, wasn't a half-bad instinct—my head's partly cloudy and I'm not really lost or confused. Today is Sunday and Tracy car-pooled to church, the store is up the road, my son needs diapers and that's the charge I've taken on. I'll go ahead and do that, then.

When I try the car door I'm surprised to find it locked. So, I try it again. Then I try the other doors—scrambling around the car and making a horseshoe in the snow. Trunk's locked too. I didn't know a car could just go ahead and lock itself like that. Maybe I should have noted this sooner, like last night—the wagon probably locks when the car's running so that a child couldn't accidentally open the door and throw himself out, or, so that a bold napper couldn't snatch the kid while the driver idled at a light. I mean, I suppose it makes sense. I'm under the impression that everything makes sense after a while. At least, I'm hoping that. Like what to do now. Inside, the keys are in the ignition and the car is running and the exhaust is creating a low-pressure frontal system—roiling clouds and all. The snow has decided it's going to go ahead and turn me into a snowman, falling with a master plan. Inside are my cell phone, my wallet, my hat, my son, and any semblance of my good fatherhood. Outside is me getting buried. I can't recall seeing a car pass in forever. I try the door handle again. It's wrong for a car to do this to a person who needed to clear his head for a moment—needed to get out and *just think*, for a second, a person who was courteous enough to leave the heat on for his infant and slumbering son. I wonder when the hammer dropped, tumbler tumbled, the locks fell, what was I doing in that instant—regarding the sky, the one, two, three, no, two blackbirds?

Let's not panic, here. Try the handle again. Don't wonder what the Sailor Man would do should he not be dead and instead of you, fidgeting in these cold shoes.

*I'd never be in this situation*, he'd say.

"Let's just say you were, Dad."

*I'd never be in it.*

"Just a hypothetical."

*Never.*

"I'm just saying, let's just say…"

*Nope.*

Moving toward the road is difficult. Stepping is something I've taken for granted now that I have to lift high to walk. Snow has gotten beneath my socks, under my jeans, and if it could, it'd crawl north all the way. When I get to the road, it's gone. What tire tracks I made have been covered over and I could be standing in the middle of the street. No one will ever come. This is on me. Not that it's my fault—I was on the way to Wade's Grocery when Sammy started howling, crying like crazy and that incessant baby-wail distracted me. I turned down the nearest side street, a county road, a place that runs parallel to the local high school, where kids play soccer. That's where I am, by the high school a few miles from Chester Ave. where Wade's is. Fair enough, that's it then. Except Sammy Bear is sleeping and has been sleeping since I started the car—he wasn't the distraction, let's not blame the child, such a nasty habit. Everyone gets turned around from time to time.

When I get back to the car, I try the handles. If the car can automatically lock itself, perhaps it can automatically unlock itself. I don't know how much gas is in the tank—I can't see the gauge—how long I have before I'm in deeper trouble than

I'm already in. Now's when I need to be decisive. Now's not the time to wonder, again, what the Sailor Man would do—*I'd never be in this situation but if I were I'd use a fist*—or weigh the pros and the cons. Now's not the time. My body has grown numb from the cold and I'm starting to feel warm in my chest somehow that I know isn't right.

The strides I take down to the creek bed are longer than they were earlier. I slip my ring off and let it mingle with whatever change I have in my pocket, and then I dig in the snow—the caustic snow-bite feels beautifully sharp right before the burn—and find a sizeable stone.

Sam's still asleep. I'm grateful for this. Surely, he'll wake up once I've smashed the window, but it will be the crash that startles him, not me, per se—he won't see his old man hustle over to the passenger side, I don't know why I choose this as the most logical window to bust, pack snow around the rock, perhaps this will lessen the shatter, somehow, stand back and pitch the hard thing—he won't know it's me doing the damage, rather, he'll remember me as the one doing the *There, there's*, and the *It's OK, baby, it's OK, Daddy's here now, baby, it's OK.* If he can remember at all, really; I have no idea how old a person is when he can remember or how far back he can go for a recollection—certainly not as far as five months—my earliest memory, if I recall right, is when I was four, maybe, and it was Halloween, and I had on the scary-mask and was following my father out the door to go trick-or-treating and he didn't know I was behind him and let the glass door with the mouth-level brass handle close behind him and knock out my two front baby teeth—*upper-cut, haymaker, hook.* I'd had my mind on the sweet thing and instead tasted a mouthful of my own blood. If Sam's anything like me, I've still got three and a half years to get this fathering down pat.

I hurl the snow-covered semi-boulder like a shot put. The glass splinters—a spider's web, for an instant, while the stone bounces back into the snow at my feet—and then explodes. The sound is big and just like it's supposed to be. In the aftermath of the break, there's a substantial silence in which I hold my breath.

Then Sammy starts into it. His cry begins like it always does—low and quick and mournful with a twinge of self-pity. But then it takes a turn for the worse. The cry moves from wail to howl—higher pitched and desperate, and from there it moves further along into out-right blood-curl mixed with the head thrash, and then my boy hits the uncontrollable-punctuated-by-three-seconds-of-build-up just flat out scream which, even to my frozen ears sounds like he's in pain.

I quickly reach my hand inside the window, feel the warm blow, and press the automatic unlock so I can open the back door and slide next to my boy. He's full-tilt now—red-faced and *gone*. His eyes-like-mine drop serious tears and I start in: "You're OK, buddy, no, no; it's OK, you're all right, I'm sorry I scared you, that was a loud noise, huh?" And talking like this, while it doesn't help him, comforts me. I'm doing what Any-Dad would do—trying, here; "Baby, baby, baby, I know, I know." He seems to be hyperventilating and I'm thinking maybe I'll need to take him out of his seat and walk him around for a while. The cold outside, though, may exacerbate the situation; he could catch a pneumonia, the wind's biting and the snow's hell-bent on putting an end to everything. Perhaps I should just drive, just *get gone*. I don't even know if the car will make it out. I've pushed countless cars out of snow banks before, I know how to coax a vehicle—reverse-forward-reverse-forward; go—and take the boy home to his mother who should be back from church by now and by God I hope she sent something kind skyward for me.

Then I see the tiny sliver of glass embedded just under my son's left eye. I see it because he's swiping at it with his mittened hands and about to spike it further beneath the skin.

"Whoa, Sammy, don't do that, now, Son." With one hand I try to push his fists away and with the other hand, pluck the sliver. But he's gone-gone, feeling the pain and trying to shake away the sting. My hands are so-cold and useless, they will never be able to get the job done, stiff and fumbling, when I grab, I can't get the glass-splinter—it is too small and too big at the same time—tweezers would be nice, I have a pocket knife on my key chain, but that idea strikes me as perhaps the dumbest one I've had in my entire life; I'd certainly take his eye out or slit his throat and make what's really maybe just a scratch something permanent and I want nothing permanent here, I'd like to get beyond the now and never ever return—when he's ten and wants to play soccer in these fields, I'll say, *No, no; let's go up the road.*

I use both hands to grip his head, say forcefully, "Hold still," and lean in with my mouth and my teeth and use my tongue a little for guidance, and I get the damned thing out and spit it away. And this sends him into some kind of melt-down. The blood that comes out of the wound is more red than I've ever seen, nothing like the dark kind that comes out of me, I work the kind of job where the once-a-week injury is part of the wage so I know what my blood looks like and it's not like Sammy's here so super-red and bright—not unlike how I remember my father's, unfortunately—and I wipe-it-away and wipe-it-away again and when it doesn't stop and starts to smear like war-paint, I guess I'll just let it bleed. Maybe I can get home before Tracy and make believe this morning never happened.

I open the passenger-side door and brush away as much glass as I can. Then I'm back in the driver's seat and notice the *all-wheel drive*, and I rock us forward, I rock us back, Sammy's scaring away the bird's outside and maybe waking the hibernating frogs back under the ice at the creek, and I start whistling loudly, to maybe distract him and it isn't until I've got the car in motion and am backing out and into what I want to believe is the road that I realize the tune I'm whistling is that damned *Popeye* song and I'm nowhere near where I want to be.

By the time I arrived home the bleeding stopped and Sam's crying had dwindled. I wet my index finger and wiped his face relatively-clean. Then I hurried inside, hefting the car-seat out of the back, and found Tracy standing in the kitchen with a cup of something to drink. The kitchen is the finest place in our pre-fab affordable house. I laid marble tile down, surplus from a job I'd worked, and it looks wonderful. When she saw us, disheveled, she asked, "How'd it go?"

I figured she knew full well. She knows me better than I know myself. I handed the boy to her, took off my shoes to stand in my wet socks, and before she could ask about the tiny dot of blood beneath his eye, I started in: "It didn't really go well. I decided to get diapers."

"That was sweet," she said, battling a yawn. "We have an extra box under the crib."

I didn't know this.

"I'll show you."

I followed them and felt something crushing looming overhead. We walked down the short-hall, in our tiny-place with bad-carpet, dog-smell, wind-drafts, roof-leak, and banged-up hand-me-down furniture. Before it was a nursery, the room was a sizeable walk-in closet. I know a carpenter who helped me transform it into a decent space for Sam, and it is enough to hold the crib and a changing table and the two of us—Mom and Irresponsible-Dad—together.

"Something happened," I said as my wife tucked a strand of her wheat-colored hair behind her ear.

"Under there," she said and pointed a finger. I noticed she had painted her nails a bright yellow. "Looks like he got a scrape."

And all at once I felt a little blizzard in my chest and, nearly-to-tears, whispered, "I can't do this anymore."

Without missing a beat, Tracy said, "Sure you can."

I asked her to explain to me what I meant because I really didn't know. And her answer made sense—"Finances, the gloomy season, lack of sleep..."

"I have been tired."

"...baby stresses, recent orphanism, car troubles..."

"Speaking of that," I interrupted—*body-blow, upper-cut, right hook.*

"The Subaru, Simon? Come on."

"I parked under an over-hang and an icicle—as big as a leg—fell and smashed the window. And a sliver from the shatter. I got it out. No big deal?"

"We need that car," she said, not facing me.

Of course I knew this and what it meant. "I'll get dad's," I replied.

Tracy turned to me and asked, "You're ready?" with her round eyes wide and concerned.

"I yam what I yam," I answered giving over to the moment.

So I'm on my way and almost-there, well, here, now. The Subaru crunches into the drive of my childhood home which is not mine. The trash bag that I wrapped around the window-

hole is already starting to tear. The snow has stopped and some
sun nudges through the cloud-cover above and it's just past
noon and if I concentrate, I can nearly-forget this morning. I
pull as close to the detached double-wide barn-like garage as
I can, put the Subaru in park, engine running, and get out,
leaving the door open. I fish around in my pocket of change;
my hands like my hands again, slip on my ring, and grab the
car key. I lift one garage door open and there's what's mine
now—his car, what he left me—a mouse-brown colored boat-
of-a-sedan, nineteen seventy-something. Thing hasn't been
moved since he fell too sick to rise and stand for long—*four,
five, six, seven...*—but my dad was the kind of man who would
rather die than stay down for the count so I'm sure he got up
and out and turned the engine over semi-regularly for good
measure. Since he's been gone the car's been sitting cold.

When I found out this is what he decided to leave me, and
this alone, I promised myself I would never come and get it, to
spite him, somehow; let him, in whatever spirit-form he may
be in feel guilty about the kind of raw deal he'd dealt me. I
can be obstinate. But that luxury's gone, we need the damned
thing—*jab, windmill, power-house.*

As I expected the car doesn't turn over. I pop the hood and
fetch the jumper-cables; hook the batteries up right. I slide into
my father's sedan and wait a while for the life in my wife's car
to make its way to his. The smell of my father is not as faint as
I expect it to be. I can make out the cologne he used trapped in
the leather of the seats. It may very well be rubbing off on me.

Next to the sedan and hanging from a beam is my father's
worn punching bag, gray-beige and motionless like a carcass.
There's a jump rope looped around the shoulders of the bag.
The ground on that side of the garage is covered in sawdust.
The Sailor Man liked shuffling in pulverized wood for some

reason—late nights, when I was younger, from the kitchen window, through half-blinds, I'd see a few paces of the stuff trailing after him toward the house when he was done.

Someone up the street is shoveling snow, rhythmically. That sound of metal on iced concrete hurts my teeth suddenly and I'm, just-like-that remembering this morning and the window shatter and how long ago it seems, this morning on the ice over the creek, when I was prepared and ready to let my pent up bitterness toward my father for abandoning my mother go, which I did, thankfully. But if I didn't or if it has somehow found me again, here is a wonderful place, in my father's car in my father's garage within plain view of the punching bag—to just let it go; *TKO.*

Then I hear a door close, the Subaru, and because the hood impedes my vision, I don't know who's done this, although, of course I know; there's really only one person, uncle Drake. He peeks into the garage following his hollow, "Hello?" He says my name quizzically as if I could be anyone else. "Simon?"

I say, "No, uncle Drake, it's a stranger sitting in the garage stealing your dead brother's car."

"Boy, is that you?"

"It is."

"I thought it might be."

The old man is wearing long underwear beneath his ruinous coat. He could use a hat.

"To what do I owe the pleasure?" he says.

"There's no real pleasure."

"Slept well, thanks to you." Drake is having trouble looking at me straight on. The sun stands behind him, props him up. "You come for a visit? Where's Samuel?"

"I came for the car." I wait a few seconds while the old man thinks of some useless banter to offer and just as he opens his mouth I roll the key, pump the gas, and startle him with the sudden pop and roar of my father's resurrected vehicle.

"What say?" I holler, having fun, now.

He shouts something back I can't hear.

"Get a hat, Drake. I need your help."

While the old man dodders back toward the house, I have to snake a hand through the garbage bag mostly-covering the broken window to unlock the Subaru doors.

I instruct Drake to follow me in my father's car. I'm pretty sure the old man does not have a valid driver's license so I drive the Subaru fast and don't wait at yellow lights, forcing him to move in a way he doesn't feel comfortable, thinking, maybe, a cop might intervene, punish the old man, a thing I'm sure he deserves. But it's Sunday and nobody cares and the roads are messy and my father's car is sturdy and could drive itself, really; Drake's just a passenger with his decrepit hands on the wheel momentarily. We head east into the industrial section of town to the auto mechanic who is over-charging me on the radiator which he had to order to fix my pickup. I'll leave the Subaru and call him tomorrow and inquire how long it will take for him to rip me off and replace the busted window. Then I shoo old Drake into the passenger seat and I'm behind the wheel of Sailor Man's car and from here on out I'm going to start thinking of it as my car since it is.

"Drives smooth," Drake says.

And this is the part that I dread the most, being in the car with my uncle, this ten-minute-drive, with him, a sentence I'll need to serve. He's got more in him. His lip is quivering and the hat that he chose to put on his head, a baseball cap labeled with a cheap beer company, completely inappropriate for the weather—not at all what I had in mind for him—is too small, it needs adjusting, and he's grinding his knees against each other and gearing up for more to say.

I wonder all at once what station my father had on his radio. What was the last song he heard before dying? When I turn the radio on, it's static and before I can crank it loud enough to drown uncle Drake, he starts in: "You know, I've been meaning to speak with you," he begins. And I don't want him to finish. I know what he wants to say. I don't want to hear that he feels guilty because the house was willed to him instead of me. My father moved him in several years ago when Drake pretended his legs were getting bad—a lie anyone with a half-brain could see; the lonely man just wanted attention and figured hobbling would advance this desire. And then, after I tell him, *It's fine, Tracy and I are happy where we are*, he's going to suggest that we move in with him, it is a big-enough place and he only stays downstairs—his room is where mine was when I was a kid—and, frankly, he'd love to have the company—*Samuel was always the social one*—and, maybe it has dawned on him that being alone could be forever. Truth is, I could use the house or at least the money from the house but no way am I moving in with the Sailor Man's slight spitting-image limping around down below. I've got the patience to wait my uncle's life out.

Drake clears his throat and continues, "I didn't get to talk to you last night. You left in such a rush."

"I love this song," I say, cranking the static, keeping my eyes dead ahead, trying to blow out the speakers.

Monday morning, before I leave for work, Tracy reminds me that Sam has a doctor's appointment this afternoon.

"Right. I'll take off early."

Sam's sitting in a high chair, cooing and content until I lean in for a peck on the blood-dot beneath his eye. That's when he swats me and whines.

"You remembered to transfer the baby's car seat?"

"I did," I say, lying and grabbing my lunch which I won't have time to eat now that I have to retrieve the baby seat I forgot yesterday. "See you at three."

"Two."

"Right. Oh," I add, "could you…"

"Call the mechanic about the window?"

"One step ahead of me, Sweets."

"Side-by-side, my heart," she says.

It snowed some last night. What's on the road is not enough to plow. My dad's car just glides along, perfect. Black ice means nothing in a vehicle like this one. I turn the radio static on. The white noise seeps into my head and pushes out any lingering thoughts and worries I'd maybe entertain in silence. I'm left just concentrating on the road and the nuances of driving in the right direction.

I've been working the master bathroom of a ritzy house on the west side. The owner of the house is a pudgy man whose hands appear webbed. He often holds them out as if he is keeping an invisible wall at bay. His wife is as tall-as-can-be and ducks when she passes beneath the chandelier in the foyer. I'm pretty sure she wouldn't hit her head if she didn't bend low, I've calculated the distance, it must just be some habit she's grown into.

The couple owns a million dogs. They're all Golden Retrievers and must eat bowls full of speed. They're manic. When one hurries out of the room, another one sprints into it. I know that they are different dogs because I see them passing each other, sniffing and drooling and I've heard the owners use so many names. One they call Buddy finds my crotch the moment the door is open.

"Right on time," the owner says. "Buddy, down."

"Yes," I say entering the house. "I'm punctual."

"You'll finish today, yes?" the wife asks, slinking in from the living room as she slides into a pullover.

"Maybe. Tile is not something you rush. Things need to settle."

"That means, no, honey," the husband says, chuckling, hands extended—pushing away nothing.

"I'll lay the tile down this morning and come back tomorrow to grout it. Don't walk on it tonight." I swat a different dog that has decided to chew on my shoe.

When I'm upstairs and mixing the mud, I realize that I've forgotten my kneepads in my wife's car. Crawling around without them is murder. It's a kind of pain that, after a few hours, I learn to appreciate. I will not be able to walk well this afternoon and I'm fine with this. I spend a substantial portion of my day on my knees and, since I'm in position—half the problem with praying is getting down low—there's no reason I shouldn't do it more often. And wear the kneepads less. God probably listens more closely to those inflicting pain upon themselves.

I set my trowel aside, close my eyes, say, *Show me how to let him go*, mustering as much emotion as I can and feeling the weight on my bony kneecaps. *I forgive him, let me forget him.*

I hold my position a few moments while God works his magic—erases the hate, inserts love—and this feels good, like maybe, with guidance from above, if I wasn't completely over him before, I'm genuinely beyond the Sailor Man now and can get on with my life, become a better husband and father and nephew and set tile straighter—I will do my best work here and remember this master bathroom as the place where I came to terms with the unresolved and whenever the owners enter to do their business they will be treading on hallowed ground.

Then one of the younger dogs licks my ear and I open my eyes and see tiny paw prints in the mortar where the puppy prances.

By working through lunch, I finish for the day around one. The owners are gone and have left me to lock up and slide the house key into a fake rock which rests atop a pile of snow. I cram the dogs in and slam the front door hard and hear them all howl as they try to make me feel guilty for leaving.

The mouse-brown-colored sedan feels good to get into and I'm off, on my way to the auto shop. I find it curious how comfortable I am in the car—considering how vehemently I promised myself I would never claim it—and how I cannot smell my father's cologne anymore. I'd like to believe this indicates a kind of growth. Acceptance and progress. After all, there were good times with my father in this car. I know, with a little effort, I can Sunday-drive down Memory Lane: recall when he took mom and me bowling or to the lake or the drive-in to watch *Rocky* sequels or to the ballgame or to *Huey's* for dinner, a place he treasured because he was worshipped there, everyone knew him, there is a spinach lasagna named after him, splendorous pictures of him on the wall, and people there covet the Sailor Man, a *Man's man*, a hero, a patriotic purveyor of good, like Popeye but *real* and boy-were-they-sad when he passed, swarms of strangers attended the wake, a few dozen old-timers made up tee-shirts with dad's fighter's-face silk-screened to wear during the ceremony, even former arch-enemies from the ring who'd been beaten by my father waited in line to say improbable-things into the microphone at the wake, clichés meant to tap into the glory of his life, so many talkers, so many references to my father, the Champ, buried with his best welter-weight belt and all kinds of mementos mourners dropped into the casket to go down with him—a mouthpiece, a ring, a tooth he'd lost someone had kept, a brass key—I eyed the women who broke down in their heavy-makeup and dark clothes with their slouched posture hunkering over his prone and slightly-smiling corpse, some leaned down to kiss his forehead and his body took on the perfume of those many different women before professionals sealed the deal and planted him in the ground, next to mom, who's funeral brought fifteen people, including my father who sat stoically and consulted his watch and waved away the minister when asked if he had anything he'd like to say—the funeral home had to extend its hours so that all the people who wanted to pay their respects to my dad were given due time and as wave after wave of sympathizers clapped my shoulders and earnestly pursed their lips at me with watery, veined eyes—*jab, hook, body-blow, round-house*—my blood boiled and my knees just about buckled. But, see, these are not the good-things I had in mind and I'm not sure where I am anymore. There are semi-trucks surrounding me—one in front, one behind, and two to the sides—and we're stopped at a light and maybe I should kill the engine and sit here buried in metal a while. When the light changes and the trucks lumber forward I follow and discover I'm heading down a street that isn't familiar until I see signs for the bus and, well, I'm pulling into the station—delivered.

I park where I can see the vending machine. It's positioned just outside the bleak terminal where it can be accessed by people stepping off the bus and those arriving from the parking lot. The machine is decorated with an enormous, wide-eyed M&M caricature and it purports to sell soda, candy, and chips. Black and yellow lettering has faded in the elements. I can tell, even from where I'm sitting, that one of the buttons is permanently depressed. At the bottom of the machine, someone has kicked in the plastic. The whole thing is canting, exhausted. I wonder how much money's in it.

Nearby, beneath a bare tree, there's a snow-covered bench. That's where the Sailor Man spent his time watching, clenching and unclenching his fists in anticipation of his next bout, pantomiming his lines, shadow-boxing the concrete sidewalk while mom was shaking and sputtering through la-la, alone.

And I have no idea where I was when he was here. There's a good chance I was on my knees counting out the hours to lunch, to quitting time, week's end, retirement; whatever. I was working, doing my job, providing—nobody's hero, nothing special. And on those infrequent occasions when lonely ladies make half-hearted passes at me I keep my head down, avert my eyes, never entertain any funny business. And I wouldn't *do* anything if they did press harder—this is a thing my wife and maybe son, when he's older, can depend upon.

I get out and pocket my keys. My bruised knees are there to remind me that I won't be walking well anytime soon. An icy gust of wind weaves through the parking lot and converges around me. I turn the collar of my shirt up and let the air guide me forward and into the station.

The middle-aged man behind the ticket counter glances up from a newspaper he's got spread out before him and frowns at the cold I'm letting in as I struggle to shut the door. He's wearing headphones and is listening to something on his Walkman radio. A woman wearing a heap of trash slumped in a plastic chair, a bum weathering it out, stirs. No way is she going anywhere today. Otherwise the terminal is empty. I tug on the door and get it closed. The lighting in the place immediately puts anyone under it into a battle against severe depression.

There are a few blinking bulbs buzzing overhead. In the corner, beneath a mute television with a horizontal line racing from top to bottom, bottom to top, is a battered pay phone. Next to the phone a garbage can is over-flowing. The builders have chosen the cheapest linoleum they could find to slap on the floor—something vomit-colored and ready to bear stains. On the walls are yellowed maps of the state and a smudged bus schedule. A sign indicates bathrooms down a short-hall.

This is where my father spent a good chunk of his time in the twilight of his life. Something must have rattled loose upstairs for him to come here—one too many shots to the head. If I would have tracked him down here when he was still alive things might have been different between the two of us. Back when he was alive, before Samuel was born, in the summertime, I could have arrived here and lifted him up by the elbow and gently guided him back home, or over to the ballpark, or down to the river to watch ducks. Or, I could have yanked him out of the chair by an ear and pummeled him, *right, left, jab, upper-cut, hook*, at his age even I could take him—*eight, nine, ten*. If I'd only done *something* maybe I would be closer to feeling nothing now.

But I've already been through this. I've let the anger go, I've let it go again and I'm not going to stand here and beat myself up anymore.

On my way to the door I catch the man behind the ticket counter glaring at me like I am responsible for all of the misery in the world. When I catch his eyes, he bends his head. I change directions—mid-stride—and step up to the counter.

I blow into my hands and say, "Cold one out there."

Because he is wearing headphones the man has the luxury of pretending he doesn't hear this. He takes his time folding the paper improperly before turning his attention to me.

"You listening to?" I ask.

"Nothing," he says and I see that he's got gum in his mouth that he hasn't been chewing. "Radio's broken. Even if it weren't there's no reception in here."

I can't exactly say for sure, from the sound of his voice, if this is the man who left the nasty messages on my father's answering machine. I'll need to hear him curse to really tell.

"Where to?" he asks.

"No where special. You recommend anyplace?"

He cocks his head and narrows an eye, quick to suspicion. His body is suddenly wracked by a tremor which could be a nervous tic, some kind of palsy, or else a shiver from the cold I held the door for. "What do you mean?"

"Where would you go if you could leave?" I ask.

"I'm not sure I understand."

"You read the obituaries?"

"How's that?"

"Got an extra piece of gum?"

"Gum?"

"I'll bet you didn't get it from the machine outside."

"It's for my smoking. It tastes like shit. Are you going to buy a fucking ticket or what?" he asks.

"Ha!" I say, certain it's him. "It's you."

And I know that this is the moment I've been waiting for—now is when I roll up my sleeves, spit out of the corner of my mouth, say, *I've had all I can stand and I can't stands no more!*, reach over the counter and deck the son of a bitch—lay him out cold. I am the Good Guy here defending the honor and dignity of Dead Dad. Whatever issues my father and I have should stay between my father and me—I don't need any help hating him.

The man curls his lip, waiting indifferently to see what I'll do. I almost think he wants me to hit him. There's not an ounce of fear showing on his face. Maybe this guy looked forward to leaving the heated messages on my father's answering machine—it was the highlight of his day, an outlet, a measured disappointment he depended upon. I'll bet he was crushed when it wouldn't take his calls anymore.

"No," I say. In relaxing, I realize that my shoulders had tensed and my fists clenched. "I'm here about the vending machine."

The man's body shudders again and he rises from his chair to square himself to me. He puts a newspaper-stained hand to his chin. "You the guy?" he asks.

"I am," I say.

We both stand quietly under the buzzing lights as a bus pulls in.

"That machine's empty," the man says. "I tried every button."

"I know," I reply, taking out my wallet, calculating how much I can afford to lose. "Let me reimburse you."

# ECHO

You know certain inexplicable things about what it means to live; you can read, you understand the difference between hot and cold, you watch images on television and laugh when they play the laugh track, you know when to eat, to sleep, to go to the bathroom. You need to go to the bathroom. You get up from bed, fully dressed, stumble instinctively into the hallway and without much trouble you find the toilet. Above the toilet is a note taped to the wall which reads, *Time to take your pills?* You don't know the handwriting. You wash up and see yourself in the mirror. You are old, that is plain enough.

There are many things that you don't know. You don't remember. What are you supposed to do today? There is something important, you're sure, on the edge of your memory. You go back to bed and try to sleep but you cannot. You must have slept well last night. The last time you remembered a dream was long ago. Sunlight from the window finds your age-speckled hand and lingers. You wear an unadorned gold ring and it looks strong on your finger. You rise from bed again and see a note taped to the nightstand reading, *Make the bed.* You tug and straighten, but the sheets won't cooperate and you tuck at all the wrong places. You leave things crumpled.

The dining room has an organ against the back wall next to a window. Outside, you see an alley and a chipped brick building. There is a cartoonish hamper-man painted in orange and blue on the side of the building. He is waving and winking. Steam blows silently into the narrow slice of morning sky. Next to the organ is a dark-wooden hutch containing glass jars half-filled with colorful hard-candies. There is a small card table and two chairs with vinyl yellow-flowered seats. The table is set for two, one paper plate heaped with cold food and the other nearly empty. A tomato with a half-peeled skin sags in a dish next to a porcelain salt shaker.

You gather the food and walk out of the dining room, past a set of stairs, and into a small kitchen. You forget why you came in here and then see the old food in your hands. The dish goes in the sink; the salt shaker belongs above the stove. Near a window is a trash can. You set the paper plates in and see a note taped to the window.

*Toss the trash out into the dumpster below.*

The window opens easily, you feel your muscles harden as you drop the contents of the can out. The air is warm and you can hear birds over the hum of the Laundromat next door. You'll go for a walk. There is a door in the kitchen. You open it and see canned vegetables and preserves on shelves. There is another door and it is locked. God knows where the key is. You think you hear movement on the other side so you press your ear to the door. Laughter? No, nothing. Maybe the wind. An animal or your imagination. Once there was a big orange tabby cat named Pinstripe or Pinetree and you were on a farm and red ants came churning up out of the earth faster than you could mash them with your sneakers and Pinstripe jumped high in the air and dashed around a green shed and disappeared.

"Pinstipe," you say, and are certain.

You have a taste for coffee. On the stove is a kettle. Someone has already filled the kettle with water and you think this is nice but you don't know how long it has been sitting there and you like your water fresh. You empty the kettle and begin to refill it in the sink. Where do you keep the coffee and sugar? You do take it with sugar, don't you? A little sugar rings a bell.

First you'll get the stove lit, and then you'll locate the coffee and sugar. Nothing happens when you twist the stove's knobs. You don't smell a hint of gas. You open the oven and look inside though you don't know what good this will do. The oven isn't working either.

In the sink water spills down the side of the overfilled kettle. It has had enough. You turn the faucet off and carry the kettle to the stove. You'll just heat the water and have a cup of coffee. How do you take your coffee? With a little sugar, for taste. When you try, the burners won't light. The stove seems to be broken. You try all the knobs and check the oven. Nothing. On the counter, in the lazy Susan, are crackers and bread. The sugar could be in one of the drawers.

A clock startles you with its chiming. You know there is something important you need to do today. You follow the sound of the clock into the living room. There are colorful pictures all over the walls. The grandfather clock in the corner falls silent. Near the front door a couch rests and a recliner lounges in front of a television. Sit in the recliner for a moment. Your skin is familiar with the soft brown fabric. On the armrest is a remote control with a note; *Push this button* taped to it. When you do as instructed the television comes to life.

Large men and women are fidgeting in plastic chairs. They speak loudly and at once.

"You don't understand," one woman says, "it's like food is our friend."

"Do you want to stop?" you hear a female voice say, though you cannot see her.

The men and women readjust themselves.

"Don't you want real friends, friends who don't disappear after you've finished eating them?" You see a svelte woman waving her arms amongst an applauding audience.

You would like to tell the big people that things will work out. It upsets you that one of the women has mascara on her blouse. If you were there you'd wipe it off. You'd try to put your arm around her and give her a handkerchief. You'd let her know that everyone eventually gets thin in the grave so eat and be merry now. But the big people are obviously upset. They slouch in their chairs and fold arms over their bellies. The camera zooms in on a man with a pensive face whispering. Then the host smiles knowingly at you and hopes you will stay tuned. The television is filled with a huge and twirling bottle of soda. "Are you thirsty?" someone asks. You might be. You can't remember if you've had your coffee yet. Before you can think this through a man wearing a yellow hard-hat named *The Anvil* appears and asks if you or someone you love has been injured in an auto accident. Didn't you lose everything you ever loved to a car crash? Maybe. The Anvil looks concerned. Where did you park your car? The keys are around here somewhere. If the weather's nice this afternoon you'll go for a ride, visit a friend.

Your eyes drift to the painting above the television. Inside the brown frame is a white church on a small hill with a blue sky. You were married in a church like this one. Your wife wore an ivory-colored dress and a veil. The minister had bad breath and you and your wife laughed about this on your honeymoon.

The show returns and the television drones and you drift off.

When you awake you have to go to the bathroom. As you struggle to get out of the chair you see the remote control on the armrest with a note taped to it. On the television something dramatic is happening. A woman says, "God, Scott, you wouldn't!" in a way that makes you hope he doesn't. You press the button and the television dies.

After you've done what you needed to do, you consider the bathtub. You'll take a bath. The water runs, you find some soap and shampoo. You take off your pants and unbutton your plaid shirt. Naked, you notice you're a mess. It isn't enough that your face is burdened by age. Across your indented chest is a thick scar in the shape of an askew number sign. You finger the pink discolored lines and feel a low pain, the type of sensation that doesn't cause alarm, instead it gives you a sinking suspicion there is something wrong with your heart. There was something wrong with your heart years ago, enough for a triple bypass, but you don't have any way to remember this, you were well sedated. There is a dark pencil mark on your left forearm where someone has written the word "Tom," and something more you can't make out. Tom could be anyone. You don't spend much time considering your genitalia so your gaze falls to the floor and your crooked feet. They are turned toward each other as if you had a magnet in one big toe and a piece of heavy metal in the other. There is a name for this, you know, you've lived with it, it kept you from the war: bird-footed? dove-heeled? crow-toed? Something like that. You never could keep up in these feet, children ran circles around you in your youth.

With effort, you draw the bath to a suitable temperature by keeping one arm in the water and using the other hand to adjust the knobs. Then you are in and it is so nice. This was a wonderful idea. You splash and lather yourself and blow bubbles and generally have a good time. When the water starts to get lukewarm, you turn a knob, the wrong one, that's *cold*; you adjust the other handle which is right and the water comes out hot and warms you and eventually you start to prune. Then there is pounding from somewhere and it startles you enough to think maybe it's your heart and then maybe it's your imagination. Accompanying the pounding you hear a muffled voice.

Reluctantly, you step from the water, wrap a towel around your midsection, and shuffle into the living room and the front door. Someone is visiting. After fumbling with the lock, you open the door and see two young women at the bottom of the stone steps.

"Hello?" you say, moving out onto the porch.

"Every time," a young woman with braces says, "like clockwork."

"Come again?" you say.

"How many times have I told you to wear a shirt when you come to the door?" the young woman with braces asks. She is dressed in a baggy shirt-sleeved shirt and jeans.

"I'm afraid you have the wrong house," you reply.

"You don't remember us."

"Sure, I do," you say, because you don't want to hurt anybody's feelings.

"Good. Then you'll remember that I'm Marcy and this is Sunny and I'm here to take care of you as always, and Sunny's here to drop of your weekly medications. Like every week. Right, Sunny?"

Sunny says, "Right." Sunny doesn't have braces, but her teeth, which you see as she recklessly chews a piece of gum, are crooked and in need of some help.

You say, "Fine."

"And," Marcy says, "it's your move, Sunny."

Marcy sets a brown paper bag on the top step at your feet and withdraws a small notepad and a pen. The young women study the notepad.

"It's going to be another cat's game," Marcy says.

"Why should I bother going?" Sunny asks.

"Because I'll go if you don't and have three O's across and you'll owe me five bucks."

The day is bright and a car passes slowly on the street in front of your house.

"I knew he wouldn't be wearing a shirt today."

"He'll learn."

You ask the girls how school is going.

Sunny climbs the steps quickly, which makes you nervous enough to clutch the cinched towel around your waist and retreat a half step. She holds a small white bag out.

"Here's your medication, Pops."

When you cautiously take the bag Sunny leans forward and deftly slashes your chest with her rough fingernail. She jumps back down the stairs and sprints up the sidewalk yelling, "X for the block, X for the block," between spurts of laughter.

You put your hand over your heart with the paper bag in a fist. Your towel starts to slip as you fall back into the house, tugging the door behind you, and slump to the floor. Your heart rattles the sack as you try to catch your breath. When you pull your hand away, you see the red X scratched above your left nipple and just outside the scar. The young women have been playing tic-tac-toe on you. Luckily, her nail didn't break the surface of your skin and even as you rub the mark, it starts to fade.

Behind you the doorknob shakes and you lean everything you have against the door.

"Your food," the young woman says, "don't forget your food. Let me just put it inside."

By lifting yourself slightly with your legs you're able to pull the towel around and re-cover your midsection.

"Don't be mad at us for playing a little game on you. You like checkers. We'll play tomorrow or the next day when I have a little more time. Open up, now, please. Here, listen. *Mares eat oats and does eat oats and little lambs eat ivy*," the woman sings softly.

You have never known how to hold a grudge. You were never strong-willed enough for it. And, truth be told, you like the sound of her voice. It is gentle, even through the door. Your breathing evens. The clock doesn't startle you as it chimes toward noon. You haven't been injured and you could handle a little company. The air fills your lungs and you feel confident enough to get up off the floor, inhaling deeply again, and face the music.

You open the door and see Mindy or Sherry or whoever it is that has the braces with a large brown bag in her hands.

"You girls should be ashamed of yourselves," you say.

"I know," the young woman says, pushing past you and into the house. "Forgive us?"

It is all you can do to get out of the way.

"Why don't you put some clothes on while I fix your lunch?"

You stand holding the front door. The day is bright and a siren from a fire engine sounds in the distance and starts to get louder as it approaches you. You close the door.

"Hello? I'm talking to you. Get in here, please," the young woman calls.

You discover her standing in your bedroom with arms crossed.

"You didn't make the bed."

Sheets are in disarray on your bed.

"Can you see this note?"

You blink a few times.

"It says, *Make the bed.* We went through this yesterday. This time, you're going to do it by yourself. Pull down the comforter and straighten the sheets."

You do as your told. For the most part, under her scrutiny, you get it right.

"My boyfriend never makes the bed. Do I need to tell you how inconsiderate that is?"

You fluff the pillow.

"It is such a simple gesture." The woman opens drawers in your dresser as you smooth out the comforter.

"Dress, and come eat."

You put on slacks, a plaid shirt, socks with red stripes at the toes, and brown shoes.

The dining room has an organ against the back wall next to a window. Outside, you see an alley and a chipped brick building. There is a cartoonish hamper-man painted in orange and blue waving and winking. On a small card table is a sandwich and a glass of milk.

"Sit down and eat."

There is a young woman in the kitchen.

"It's peanut butter and raspberry jelly. I pulled the crusts off."

You sit and take small bites and chew thoroughly like you've always chewed.

*"A kid'll eat ivy too, wouldn't you?"* the woman sings from the kitchen. "Maybe tomorrow I'll bring you an ivy sandwich?"

You have no idea what the woman is talking about so you say, "Fine."

"You still like that song, right? I play it for you sometimes?"

When you get thirsty, you drink some milk. Although the sandwich tastes good, it is tricky, a few nagging raspberry seeds get trapped in your teeth and you try to unlodge them with your tongue. The young woman joins you in the dining room.

"I put some cold meatloaf and a salad in the refrigerator for later. Again, you didn't eat the tapioca pudding. Your wife told us it was your favorite, why don't you eat it?"

"I'll eat it," you say.

"Have it after dinner."

"Fine," you say.

"I put your pills in the medicine cabinet, remember to take them later."

"Fine."

"Fine, yes, everything's *hunky-dory*. It won't be *fine* if you don't start trying to take care of yourself a little harder. You can't count on me for everything."

The woman raps her knuckles on your head.

"If you go outside, fasten yourself and don't wander into the neighbor's yard again," she says.

"I won't," you say.

"Have a good day and I'll see you tomorrow. And, I'm sorry if Sunny scratched you. Next time wear a shirt."

The raspberry seed will not come loose so you work on it with your finger.

The young woman walks into the kitchen, returns with a toothpick, hands it to you, pats you on the shoulder and leaves. You hear the front door open and close.

You tell yourself to remember a shirt. You wonder who the young woman is in relation to you. She is a nice girl, you think, a bit bossy, but friendly. She has a nice voice, like your wife.

Your wife, Francis. You call her Francis-June because she has a birthday in June and it is your secret way of remembering.

You are grateful for the sandwich and the toothpick. The seeds come free and you swallow them down.

In the bathroom you find water in the tub that is not clean, it is not hot. You unplug the drain and listen to the water complain as it circles away. The window in the bathroom looks out into your neighbor's side yard. Against the house is a tomato garden. The vines are heavy with the burden of fruit. Or vegetable. You can't remember if a tomato is a fruit or a vegetable. Vegetable makes the most sense somehow. When you leave the bathroom you remember that you didn't do anything while you were in there and decide that you didn't need to go after all.

The dining room table has an empty plate and a glass. You gather these things and move into the kitchen. The glass goes in the sink, the paper plate in the trash.

*Toss the trash out into the dumpster below.*

The window opens with a little difficulty. You feel your muscles strain as you drop the contents of the can out. The air is warm and you hear traffic over the hum of the Laundromat. You'll go for a drive, see your friend Calvin. You remember Calvin. The two of you could have a beer and talk baseball. You can't recall where Calvin lives or how the Cubs are doing, but you'll figure that out once you're in the car and on the road. The radio might have the game on. Listen to the radio first and then give Calvin a call and meet him at *Ronny's* for a drink. You open a door in the kitchen and search for the radio. Canned vegetables and preserves. There is another door and it is locked. You think you hear music on the other side, but the radio's upstairs, isn't it?

The stairs are just around the corner. You take them slowly and with your arms splayed to the sides for balance. You know better than to hurry up stairs. If you fell, who would pick you back up? Francis-May, you guess. Francis-June? Your wife. You don't know when she'll be back, don't know where she went. Probably the beauty parlor with one of her friends.

Upstairs the front room has model airplanes suspended in flight by fishing line attached to the ceiling. You see propeller planes with fancy tiger-striped wings or cockpits streaked with flames, and elaborate bombers angled in slow-banked turns, their exposed bellies weighted with oblong missiles. You identify a Helldiver, A Curtiss P-40, A Piper, a Taylorcraft, and a Douglas B-19. These are your planes.

Against the back wall, on a bookshelf, you see a black and white photograph propped in a cracked frame in a patch of dust. The shot shows two men smiling with arms around each other; one man in uniform with a chin like a brick, the other dressed in civilian-wear and a baseball cap. For a moment you are the airforce pilot who fought in World War II; you imagine the smoldering city below and the tiny tanks engaging each other as you maneuver the skyway above. The many war films with the jet-fighting scenes have left a convincing imprint on your memory. You are not the uniformed man in the picture, however. That was your brother, Alexander. Your Dad called him Alley Cat because he had been tough. You used to rumble with him, he was older, that's what he wanted to do. Once, you broke his pinky finger and it changed your life. You shouldn't have focused all of your strength on that one weak finger, it was a malicious thing to do. Alexander was fine, he had a splint for a while, but you snapped his trust. He stopped horse playing with you and found his calling in the war. Your arm around his shoulder was a pose for the picture.

Don't let this upset you. Sit down and collect yourself in the rocking chair in the corner.

On the floor beside the chair is a book, *The Odyssey*, creased at page twenty-five, probably where you left off. You pick it up from there, but you are lost and go back to the beginning. You rock and read and nod and nod until the book succeeds in slipping to the floor.

When you awake you are disoriented by the unsteady rocking chair. Your shirt collar is moist with a circle of drool. You need to use the bathroom.

You choose the wrong way to the stairs and step into the small loft in the upper corner of the house. The room is filled with light from the many windows and the bright colors on the walls hold the sunshine inside. Short containers of paint are stacked in neat rows among canvases and brushes. Rolling fields and turgid ocean waves and delicate winter streets adorn the many paintings leaning against the walls, some framed, others unbound. You know better than to think this work is yours.

Close to the window is a canvas clothes-pinned to an easel. There is an oval-shaped mirror hanging from the wall in front of the painting. You look at yourself, old with deflated cheekbones and insignificant eyes among the pinches of soft skin, in need of a shave.

On the canvas is a portrait of a young woman from her collarbone up. You recognize her as your Francis-June. Her brown eyes are sharp with flecks of gold and the way they gaze back at you makes you wonder if she is about to reveal a secret or laugh out loud. She is like that. She makes you want to guess what she is thinking, makes you care what is on her mind. Her hair touches her shoulders and has a tinge of red you don't remember. Her lips are perfectly reproduced, you half expect her to speak. You can see a little teeth peeking out between them. Your wife takes great pride in her teeth. When you were first married she had a ritual of flossing and brushing every night before bed and she visited the dentist more often than you thought necessary. Regardless, you felt a comfort in her dental care, as if she were cleaning for you too. Her chin and forehead and cheeks are painted an alabaster-white that is paler than you remember. You recall a flush of olive in her skin that has been extracted in the portrait. You don't mind, though. The lighter shade makes her look crisp and new, perhaps like she looked the first time you saw her.

You wish your wife were here so you could tell her that this picture is beautiful but not as beautiful as the real thing.

Through trial and error, you locate the bathroom and relieve yourself. You look out the window into your neighbor's side yard where he or she has planted a tomato garden against the side of the house. The vines are heavy with the burden of fruit. Or vegetable. The blinds in a window next door part and you step away to avoid being seen.

*Time to take your pills?*

You don't know how to answer that question. It could be time to take your pills. Behind the mirror is a medicine cabinet. On one of the shelves is a small water glass with a set of teeth resting in old water. These are not your teeth, yours are still in you mouth. You take the glass out and shake it. Bits of orange and red food swirl in the water like a globed Christmas-thing. Tomato skin. These are your wife's teeth and those are pieces of tomato skin. Francis-June loves tomatoes, always has. Ever since her dentures, though, she has had trouble with the skin. It would be nice of you to pick a couple of tomatoes for supper tonight from the garden outside. You'll leave a few dollars for your neighbor, they won't mind. Where did you put your wallet? Probably in the bedroom, on the nightstand. First, though, put the cup of teeth back in the medicine cabinet.

You walk into the dining room. There is an organ against the wall. You sit on the small bench in front of the organ and try to play but no sound comes out. You spend several minutes trying to turn it on and then give up. Your wife used to play a song, you don't remember the words, but you remember the tune. Where is Francis-May, Francis-June? Today could be her birthday. That's what you've been forgetting all day. You better get her a gift, bake her a cake. But maybe it's not her birthday. If it isn't, you'd look silly with a birthday cake, egg on your face. No need to overdo it. Something simple would be thoughtful even if it isn't her birthday. Go get her a book or a new paintbrush.

Next to the organ is a dark-wooden hutch containing glass jars half-filled with colorful hard-candies. You open the cabinet doors and dig in. The candy is clumped together and impossible to break into pieces. You keep at it, though.

Then the phone rings, you think. You hold steady, with your hand in the glass jar. The phone rings definitely. It takes you some time to untangle your hand from the candy jar and close the glass hutch and since your hand is sticky you don't know how to answer the phone. You don't even know where the phone is. Follow the ringing into the living room. On a small table next to the couch you see the phone which has gone silent. You pick it up anyway, with your left, non-sticky hand.

A dial tone answers.

You were hoping it was Francis. Put the receiver down and rest on the couch for a minute, catch your breath. You have a clear view out the front window into the front yard and street. Outside, cars pass, and you lean an inch forward with each passing one by one until your chin is at your chest and you're under.

Twilight is a difficult time. You stiffly wake into it for no reason. Nothing particular pulled you from sleep, no urge and no distraction. You don't know why you fell asleep, but it is more bothersome that you don't know why you woke up. As you rise to stand at the window your mood dims. The tree in your front yard is green and full. A squirrel fidgets near the sidewalk and the crimson light holds for a moment on its tail before it flits back into shadows. A porch light goes on at the house across the street and a few doors down you see a thin woman in a suit shade her eyes as she leafs through the mail at her mailbox. The cars don't know whether to turn their head-lights on. A red fire hydrant at the curb is ablaze in sunlight. You don't like this. The light doesn't seem to be your light at all. You have half a mind to run out and shout the sun away from the curb. Hell, why not do this?

You fiddle with the lock on the front door, which isn't locked, but you lock it and then unlock it and when it is open part of your gusto's gone and the steps you take onto the front porch are tentative ones. You've forgotten how intimidating the sky can be spreading away as it does. The cars are louder than you remember. Somewhere a lawnmower chokes and starts and it sounds so much like a machine, you think, you can picture the motor grinding, the blades indiscriminately churning for-ward. By the time you get to the curb, the sun is down and you forgot what you rushed out here for in the first place. A man holding a baby waves to you across the street and asks you something you can't really hear.

"Fine," you say, waving back.

Then the phone rings, you think.

"I've got to get that," you call to the man, who is actu-ally carrying a bag of groceries, and he seems to think this is a good idea, you answering the phone, he bows slightly and nods. And then it is important for you to get inside the house and assume the responsibilities that come with owning a phone and receiving a call.

If the phone was ever ringing, it is not by the time you return inside. The clock is making noise, like it has all day, marking the hours. You grab the phone anyway and notice that your hand is sticky, somehow.

A dial tone answers. You put the receiver in the cradle.

In the bathroom, you wash your hands with soap. When you see your face, your heart skips a beat. You don't remember yourself so old. The stubble of your gray beard looks hideous. You need a shave.

After some adjusting, you find the proper water temperature; a hint of steam begins to fog the bottom of the mirror. You roll your sleeves up and look around for shaving cream and a razor. Above the toilet is a note which you don't bother reading, and behind the mirror, in the medicine cabinet, you find a cup of water with dentures in them. There are flecks of red food that stir when you move the cup, like an unsettled snow globe, and you know the teeth aren't yours, they belong to Francis, bits of tomato, she loves tomatoes but has trouble with the skins. Behind a wall of amber-colored pill vials is a razor.

You lather your face with soap and start to shave. Francis doesn't think you are as ugly as you do. In fact, she claims you resemble a Greek god, or somebody mythical. She loves myths. The name she calls you is her Hercules? her Achilles?

Next door somebody turns on a light and it distracts you to the window. There is a garden in the neighbor's side yard and in the semi-dark the tomatoes have lost their color.

You finish shaving and wash the soap away. The face in the half-steamed mirror looks younger without the whiskers; bearable and wearable, you suppose. Adonis. That is the name Francis-June calls you sometimes, her Adonis.

*Time to take your pills?*

Yes, it is time. You should take your pills. They are in the medicine cabinet. First turn off the water and put the razor away. In the medicine cabinet, the cup of teeth. Francis loves tomatoes and today might be her birthday and it would be a nice gesture if you picked a couple of ripe ones from the garden next door. Behind the stack of pill bottles is an eyebrow pencil. Francis paints her face on every morning. You have the presence of mind to write the word "tomato" on your exposed left forearm, although you forget exactly how to spell the word and just write "tom." You'll know what you mean. From a pill bottle with your name on it you palm a couple of pills and swallow them dry.

In the dining room you return to the organ and, with a little luck, find the button to click it on. You have to wait a few moments while it warms up, and in that time you thumb through a music book and try to remember something to play. If you ever knew how to read music, you have forgotten. After a while, though, by toying with the keys, your hands rediscover the tune, "John Jacob Jingleheimer Schmidt," an easy song to remember. "His name is my name too." You sing it a few times, nice and loud. The grandfather clock backs you up with its chiming.

When you have had enough of "John Jacob" you try to get "Mares Eat Oats" out, but you cannot. Francis-June knows that one best. She should be home soon, it must be suppertime by now. When you think about it, you're hungry. Also, there was something you were supposed to do other than play the organ.

Today is Francis-June's birthday, and you were going to bake her a cake. Unless it isn't her birthday, and you look like a buffoon giving her a cake when she hasn't aged a year yet. Why don't you give her something smaller and play it by ear when she comes home? She would like it if you fixed dinner tonight.

There is a salad and meatloaf in the refrigerator, paper plates on the counter, and if you wash the glass in the sink, you can get something for Francis to drink. The date on the milk carton expired in May and if today is Francis' birthday, you're already into June and even though it smells fine, you'd better get rid of it.

*Toss the trash out into the dumpster below.*

You can only manage to open the window halfway, for some reason it seems to be stuck. There is room enough to fit the can out. The air has a bit of a chill to it, refreshing, really, and you can hear the crickets over the hum of the Laundromat next door. You wonder if the stars are out. You can't see them from your kitchen. Maybe later you'll take Francis for a stroll down the block to the Dairy Queen for a Dilly Bar. She will enjoy it, especially if it is her birthday. Supper before dessert, though.

You divide the salad and meatloaf onto the two plates, there is enough, and you carry them into the dining room and the table. You'll need utensils, napkins, and something to wash the food down. Back in the kitchen, you find a glass in the sink. After rinsing it out, you look in the refrigerator but cannot find anything to drink. You thought you had milk. Water will have to do.

When the water is cold you fill the glass, carry it into the dining room and have a seat. You forgot utensils. Outside the window the hamper-man is giving you a knowing wink. You wink back, you're a fine winker, then you laugh; here you are, sitting down to dinner and winking at a painting on the wall. You belong in a nuthouse. Sometimes you tease your wife by singing, "If I had a face like Francis had, I know what I would do. I'd take myself to the county park and there I'd join the..."

What would you join? Start again.

There is a ring on your finger, strong and gold. Someone has written the word "tom" on your arm. Food is heaped on plates in front of you. You take deep breaths. Soon, you are aware that you need to use the bathroom.

Outside the bathroom window, in your neighbor's light, is a tomato garden. A tomato is a fruit and you like to eat them although you have trouble with the skin, it gets caught in your teeth.

*Time to take your pills?*

This note is for you although you don't recognize the handwriting. The pills are in the medicine cabinet, behind the bathroom mirror. Your face startles you. In the cabinet are teeth resting in a glass. Shake it and see the flecks of red. These aren't your teeth, they are your wife's, she is the one who loves tomatoes, not you, she can't eat them with skin. Where is your wife?

"Francis?" you call out.

No answer. You have a feeling you're forgetting something important. Concentrate.

It is your wife's birthday. You didn't get her anything. She isn't a picky woman. It's too late to bake a cake. If you cook dinner, maybe snatch a tomato and peel it for her, she will be delighted.

Go get a tomato from the garden next door.

It is dark. You find a switch and light your living room. Your wife could be home any moment. Hurry, now, get a tomato, then cook dinner.

Outside is too much. The clouds are knitted above forever. You stumble from the porch down into the lawn and drop. Your hands keep you from falling to your face. The grass is moist and marks your pants at the knees. This was a bad idea, you think, this was a bad idea. What are you doing here? You came out for something, maybe fresh air, and the air feels wicked against your skin. You find it hard to swallow. On your arm; "tom." This is short for tomato.

A few feet in front of you is a chain. Crawl to it, find its end, fasten the clasp to your belt loop for safety. You won't get lost. The chain is tethered to a tree and the tree is right there, in your front yard. Stand and be strong. You are a grown man. You used to fly planes, for God's sake.

The distance the chain lets you travel is to the sidewalk, short of the street, and halfway around the house. The tomato garden is illuminated by light from your neighbor's window. You march toward it, remembering Francis-June and supper tonight. Get her a tomato for her birthday. It's not a big deal, you'll tell her, she should enjoy.

The chain nearly rips your pants off as you stride ahead. You are short of the garden by fifteen feet. Where you stand, in the side yard, it is dark and the wetness at your knees gives you a chill. You are aware of your heart. "Tom," on your arm, is an old friend. Tom and Francis-June. Unfasten yourself for them and cover the distance to the garden on your own.

By the time you get to the tomatoes, you are confused. You crouch in the light, rest in the dirt. You hug your knees and rock yourself. A dog barks in the distance. You used to have a dog named Pinwheel or Pinstripe. That was a big orange-colored mutt and you were on a farm and red ants came churning up out of the earth faster than you could mash them with your sneakers and Pinstripe jumped high in the air and dashed around a green shed and disappeared.

"Pinstripe," you say, and are certain.

Your neighbor opens a window and calls out. It is an elderly woman, you see her face, but she cannot see you. You don't answer.

"I'm calling the cops," she says.

Stay calm, control your breathing. She will go away soon. When she closes the window, you relax. On your arm someone has written the word, "tom." You wrote that, it is short for tomato. Grab a tomato and peel it for Francis-June, it is her birthday.

You snag the sweetest tomato and scramble like a soldier back into your house.

Inside, you lock the front door in case anyone is after you. The tomato is huge, Francis-June is going to love it. The dining room is already set with food.

"Francis?" you call out. "Did you make dinner?"

She doesn't answer. She's probably in the bathroom. Prepare the tomato before she gets out. You search for a light switch in the kitchen. It is around here somewhere. Forget it, just wash the tomato, grab a bowl, and start peeling.

"How was your day, dear?" you say, over the sound of the running water, as you wash the tomato.

You can't be sure, but you think she says, "Fine."

"Great. Mine too."

After you dry the tomato, you find a bowl and move back into the dining room.

"You made meatloaf, great, honey," you say, sitting with your back to the hallway and the bathroom. If she comes out, you don't want her to see what you're doing.

You pull the stem from the tomato and set it aside. Then, very carefully, with your fingernails, you begin to peel the to-mato. The skin doesn't come off in easy strips, you have to work for each little piece. After a while, you expose the fleshy fruit, with the small greenish seeds and veins. That's the part your wife can handle.

You've forgotten the salt. Francis likes it with a little salt, for taste. Hurry into the kitchen and grab it; there it is on the stove.

She is still in the bathroom, you still have a lot of tomato to peel.

You start to sing "Mares Eat Oats" while you work, but you don't remember all of the words. You can hum it, though, so you do. You peel the tomato, one fingernail full of skin at a time. When you need to use the bathroom you repress your urge because Francis-June is still in there. Inevitably, you must, and you're polite enough to knock on the bathroom door even though it is not completely closed. When you see that your Francis-June is not in here, it worries you for a moment, you swore you heard her washing her hands a second ago. No matter, she'll be home soon; you relieve yourself and wash up, hating the old face looking back at you in the mirror.

You find your seat in the dining room and eat the cold food in front of you with your fingers. You don't know how supper got here if Francis-June didn't make it. After you have eaten, you lift the tomato from the dish. It is already turning soft, but the weight of the thing is substantial.